AGAIN WITH FEELING

THE LAST PICKS BOOK 6

GREGORY ASHE

H&B

This is a work of fiction. Names, characters, places, and incidents either are the product of the author's imagination or are used fictitiously, and any resemblance to actual persons, living or dead, business establishments, events, or locales is entirely coincidental.

Again with Feeling

Copyright © 2024 Gregory Ashe

All rights reserved. No part of this book may be reproduced in any form, stored in any retrieval system, or transmitted in any form by any means—electronic, mechanical, photocopy, recording, or otherwise—without prior written permission of the publisher, except as provided by United States of America copyright law. For permission requests and all other inquiries, contact: contact@hodgkinandblount.com

Published by Hodgkin & Blount
https://www.hodgkinandblount.com/
contact@hodgkinandblount.com

Published 2024
Printed in the United States of America

Version 1.05

Trade Paperback ISBN: 978-1-63621-100-8
eBook ISBN: 978-1-63621-099-5

Chapter 1

"You're leaving?" I straightened in my seat so fast that my knee jarred the table. "You can't abandon me!"

"I'm not abandoning you," Bobby said as he collected his trash.

Up until that moment, it had been a beautiful day. It was June, and the sun was shining. Don't get me wrong—it wasn't warm by any stretch of the imagination. But a year into my time in Hastings Rock, I'd finally figured out that jeans and a hoodie were *de rigueur* (I learned that word from an Ian Fleming novel about a gala!). The sky was a deep blue, empty of clouds, and from where we sat on the pier at our table in the Fishermen's Market, the glittering, restless waves seemed to go on forever. Mixed in with the smell of the ocean was the delicious fragrance of fried food—people didn't come to Fishermen's Market to go on a diet.

"But we've got to practice," I said, looking from Bobby to Fox, then to Millie, then to Indira, and even (God help me) to Keme for backup. "The sandcastle building contest is—"

I cut off because my phone buzzed. The message was from Hugo—most of my messages these days were from Hugo. Ever since we'd reconnected a few weeks before—purely from a professional standpoint—we'd been messaging a lot. About a project, if you need to know. A novel we were planning on coauthoring. Like I said, purely professional.

All his text said was *Midpoint twist: he's been dead the whole time.*

I messaged back, *You want to use that one every time.*

Because it's the best possible twist.

The intense silence, more than anything, reminded me where I was, and I was surprised to catch myself grinning.

When I looked up, Bobby asked, in a tone that could have meant anything, "How's Hugo?"

"Fine, I guess." There was no reason for my face to feel hot, but it did. "He just had an idea for the book—" I took a breath. "The sandcastle building contest is this weekend, Bobby. That's the whole point of coming out here today, to practice."

"Oh," Bobby said, "I meant to tell you. Kiefer asked me to enter the contest with him." If you didn't know Bobby, you would have thought the lack of eye contact was just an accident—that he really was too busy picking up his trash to glance over at me. "That's okay, right?"

I stared at him, unable to summon words. He still wouldn't look at me.

"It'll be fine, Bobby," Indira said. She looked particularly lovely today, that white lock of witch hair blowing in the wind, wearing a smart jumper and jeans that she insisted she didn't mind getting sandy.

Fox nodded agreement so enthusiastically that their derby hat almost slid off their head. They'd pinned a little dragon on a spring to the front, and now the dragon wobbled wildly on its perch. "Dash can be on our team."

Finally, I managed to ask, "Who?"

"Or he can be on OUR TEAM!" Millie said. In her leggings and Hastings Rock sweatshirt, and sitting as close to Keme as she was, it would have been easy to mistake them for the same age—and for a couple. Which, I'm sure, would have made Keme die from happiness.

Right then, though, the boy was scowling at me from inside his ancient hoodie (so old that the Ketling Beach Surf Shop logo had flaked away into near illegibility). He was the only one of us not wearing pants—his board shorts looked as old as his hoodie, and I didn't have to see his flip-flops to know they were cracked and splitting. He had his long, dark hair up in a bun, which had the disturbing effect of making him look almost like an adult. "No," he said, giving me a warning look. "He can't."

Millie laughed like Keme had made a joke.

"Kiefer," Bobby said, and now his eyes did come up. His tone suggested he was prompting me. "I've told you about him. He's the guy I've been going out with."

I almost said, *Which one?*

Fortunately, with the Last Picks around, I didn't have to.

"Is he the one with the squint?" Fox said.

Indira shook her head. "He's the one who owns a go-kart."

"It wasn't a go-kart," Millie said. "It was a dune buggy. But I thought Kiefer was the one who had all the tattoos."

"He has TATTOOS?" My volume verged on Millie levels for a moment.

"He's an artist," Keme said.

Bobby gave him a grateful look. "Yeah—"

"Oh," Fox said, "the one who works on the boardwalk. He does those cute little caricatures."

I've never had any romantical feelings toward Fox. Ever. But right then, I wanted to kiss them.

"That's just a gig," Bobby said, "until he gets into art school."

"God, don't let him go to art school," Fox said. "He'll have a mountain of debt and end up becoming a deep-fryer jockey."

"What is a deep-fryer jockey?" Indira asked.

"It's like a regular jockey," Millie said, "but the deep fryer is the HORSE! Wait, does Kiefer have a horse?"

Bobby checked his watch. "I've got to run."

"Oh my God, are you going on a date RIGHT NOW?"

The hint of color that rose under the olive-gold of his complexion was answer enough, but he managed to say, "Uh, yeah, Millie. I am."

"What kind of tattoos?" I asked. "Where? Are we talking flowers and mermaids? Or skulls and chains and barbed wire?"

Bobby stared at me as though I were speaking a foreign language. For that matter, so did everybody else.

"Joking," I said. "That was a joke."

Then, to seal the deal, I made myself laugh.

Everyone's eyes got huge.

A seagull screamed, did a startled take-off, and swerved at the last moment to avoid one of the piles.

At the next table, a baby started to cry.

"Okay," Bobby said slowly. "I'll see you all later." He reached out like he might squeeze my shoulder or scruff my hair, but he let his hand drop to his side again, and he left. He didn't look back.

"What is wrong with you?" Fox whispered furiously at me.

"What is wrong with *me*—" I tried.

"We're so sorry," Millie said to the tourist family at the next table, who were glaring at us. Well, at me. They were dressed in shorts and T-shirts, and the gentleman wore a sun visor that said CORNHUSKERS. "He's not usually like this," Millie continued, "but he has this friend, well, they're more than friends—"

"He actually *is* usually like this," Keme said over her, "because he's a donkey."

"Keme," Indira said.

The boy subsided back into his seat, but only to settle a glare on me. "Fix this," he said. "Now."

"Fix what?" I said. "Did you hear him? He's going to enter the sandcastle contest with—with whatever his name is, even though they just met, even though he and I have been planning our design for weeks. I mean, we're definitely going to win—it's Hogwarts after the Death Star crashes into it. How can that lose?"

"Because no one has any idea what it means," Fox snapped. "And Keme is right: you need to fix this. I think we've all been very patient, and yes, at the beginning, it was cute to see you two pussyfooting around—"

"I really don't think you can say that," I whispered. "There are children here."

"—but we're all sick and tired of it."

"Sick and tired of what?"

Indira gave me a disappointed look. Keme's glare got, somehow, even darker.

Millie, though, just burbled, "You know, you and Bobby."

"What—"

"That you LIKE each other."

"Well—"

"But you can't ever get the timing right—"

"Or you're a donkey," Keme put in.

"—and everyone knows you'd be perfect together," Millie said, "if you'd just KISS!"

The word echoed through the market. At the next table, the Cornhusker dad covered the baby's ears. And remember that poor seagull that almost hit a piling? It was perched on a hawser at that moment, and I kid you not: it. fell. off. Just rocked backward and disappeared.

Working a finger in my ear, I said, "Okay, I appreciate the concern, but Bobby and I are just friends, and we both know what's best for us—"

"No," Fox said, "you don't."

"You clearly don't, dear," Indira said.

"Definitely not," the mom at the next table said. She snorted. "Just friends? That young man couldn't take his eyes off you."

"Bobby is going through a really tough time," I said, sparing a dark look for Nebraska Mom. "He's still working through his breakup with West. I mean, they were engaged. And that was a big deal for him. He's grieving. He's processing. He's healing."

"I've heard that before," said Cornhusker Dad.

"You know," I said, "this is a private—"

"Really?" Fox asked over me. "Is he grieving, processing, and healing by slee—" They cut off and gave an embarrassed sidelong look at the family next to us. "By *courting* every eligible young man within driving distance?"

Keme still hadn't said anything, but he was still staring at me, and his look was approaching murderous levels.

"This is what he needs right now—" I started.

"No, Dashiell," Indira said. "It's not."

"Definitely not," Nebraska Mom said again, this time with a definite 'tude.

"Okay, well, I think it is." I was surprised by the sharpness of my tone, and to judge by the looks on everyone else's face, so were they. "I know you all want what's best for me and Bobby, but you're not part of our—our relationship, for lack of a better word. So, you don't understand."

As soon as I heard myself, I wanted to wince. It was such a stereotypically teenager defense that I actually thought I could feel the ghost of sixteen-year-old Dash breathing down my neck.

"Tell us," Fox said in a dangerously even voice. "What don't we understand?"

I wanted to say no. I wanted to tell them I was done discussing this. But I'd dug myself a hole, and now all I could do—it seemed—was try to dig myself out of it. "Have you ever heard of a rebound relationship?"

It was Keme who spoke this time: slowly, clearly, and dark as a bottomless pit. "You are an idiot."

"I don't have to explain myself to any of you," I said, getting out of my seat. "Bobby just needs to get this out of his system, and then things will go back to normal, and—"

But my phone buzzed again, and I checked it—a Pavlovian response.

It wasn't a message from Hugo, though. It was an incoming call.

I answered, and a prerecorded voice said, "This call is originating at the Oregon State Penitentiary from," and then another, familiar voice broke in and said two words. A name. "Vivienne Carver."

Chapter 2

"To accept this collect call, press one—" the prerecorded message continued.

My face must have shown something of what I was feeling because Indira said, "What's wrong?"

Cornhusker Dad asked—with misguided enthusiasm—"Is it Kiefer?"

"Dash?" Fox asked.

Keme sat up and glanced around, as though the threat he sensed might be physical.

"It's Vivienne," I said. "She's calling collect." And then, perhaps unnecessarily, I added, "From prison."

"Don't answer!" Millie shouted and then clapped a hand over her mouth.

Indira and Fox traded a look.

In my ear, the message was repeating itself now. I was distantly aware of a rushing sound in my head. Sweat had broken out across my back and under my arms. It took me a moment to recognize the bubble in my chest as panic, making it impossible for me to draw a full breath.

"I'm not sure it would be wise—" Indira began.

Definitely not wise, I thought. I'd moved to Hastings Rock to take a job with Vivienne; she'd been one of the best-selling mystery writers in the world, and on top of that, she'd solved a number of real-life murders. All of that, though, had been before she faked her own death and then tried to kill me.

So, why was she calling me now?

I wanted to know. And competing with the panic in my chest was an ember of anger, growing brighter and hotter as my shock faded. Before I could second-guess myself, I pressed one, and the call clicked as it connected.

I was proud of myself, by the way. My voice came out rock steady. "Hello?"

There was the slightest pause. The connection, maybe. Or perhaps Vivienne had been surprised I'd accepted the call. "Good afternoon, Dashiell."

"Just Dash," I said. "What do you want?"

She laughed. "What a way to talk, Dashiell. No longer playing the part of the wide-eyed naïf, are we?"

"What do you want, Vivienne?"

"How are you liking Hemlock House?"

"It's wonderful. It's big and beautiful and full of complicated people and fraught relationships. It's just like home. What do you want?"

"I want you to solve a murder."

I burst out laughing. Fox's eyes widened. Indira frowned. Keme looked at Millie, and Millie still had one hand over her mouth.

Until a moment later when she stage-whispered, "What does she want?"

Nebraska Mom, who was now busily wiping the baby's face and hands, said, "Yeah, the rest of us can't hear her."

"You've got to be kidding," I said into the phone. "I don't know what kind of trick you're trying to pull, but I'm not interested. Goodbye—"

"No, please!"

The words were sharp, and they had a breathy, punched-out quality, as though they'd been wrenched from her against her will.

I told myself to disconnect.

Instead, I said, "Hold on."

With a quick wave for the Last Picks, I made my way out of Fishermen's Market. The pier was busy with families and buskers and vendors—Hastings Rock was at the height of its tourist season. Mrs. Palakiko, in her enormous sunglasses, was doing steady business at her shave ice stand, and it looked like Mr. Li had set up his vendor tent on the pier today instead of the boardwalk. A pair of blond ladies with matching headbands were holding up one of his bestselling tees—ROCK ON – HASTINGS ROCK—and seemed to be considering purchasing multiples in various colors. The breeze was steady, and farther down the pier, Mr. Tate was helping a little Black girl get her kite up.

I headed in their direction—not because I wanted to help with the kite, but because the crowd was thinner at the end of the pier, and the press of people was making my anxiety tick into the red. As I walked, I said, "Okay, what's the punch line?"

"It's not a joke, Dashiell—Dash. I'm quite serious. I've been wrongly accused, and I believe you're the perfect person to prove I'm innocent."

Another laugh escaped me. "This keeps getting better and better. All right. Who are you supposed to have murdered? Besides Mr. Huggins and Sheriff Jakes?"

"My brother."

I kept walking. My steps rang out on the creaky old boards. The little girl with the kite was laughing. A pair of teenage boys were trying to feed french fries to a seagull and screaming every time it came close to them.

"Okay," I finally said.

"Needless to say—well, I suppose it's not needless, is it?" Vivienne took a breath. "I didn't kill him. I loved my brother. Deeply. I want you to prove I didn't do this; I will not be known as a kin slayer and a fratricide. And more importantly, I want you to find out who *did* kill him."

"Vivienne—" I struggled for a moment with what to say. "I'm sorry for your loss. But I don't think I'm the right person—"

"You are, though. That's why I called you. I've been keeping my eye on you, Dash, and you've outdone yourself. It's a shame things worked out the way they did because I think you and I might be kindred spirits."

If you've never had a homicidal maniac call you a kindred spirit, let me tell you, it takes the shine off your day. And I didn't love that part about *keeping an eye on you* either. But all I said was "I've helped with a few investigations, but only because—"

"It's always 'only because,'" Vivienne said, and it took me a moment to recognize the note in her voice as amusement. Wry amusement. As though she knew all too well. "It's a friend, or a friend of a friend, or a long-lost nephew."

My throat was strangely dry, but I managed to say, "No nephews."

"Let me tell you why you must be the one to investigate my brother's death. The first reason is because you're good at it. You won't settle for superficial answers. You won't accept the story that those bumbling police will embrace. Because you want to know the truth, Dashiell." Again, her tone changed—taking on an intensity that surprised me. "That's always our charge, isn't it? To see truly, to know truly, so that we may write truly. That's what carries us into the dark."

"Actually, I think I just read too much Chandler at an impressionable age."

She laughed, and it broke the unexpected tension of the moment. "Second, because my family will talk to you, Dashiell. In fact, they'll tell you everything you want to know. Because you destroyed my life once, and they will assume—gleefully—that you're trying to destroy it again. Hammer a few more nails in the coffin, that kind of thing."

"Nice family."

"You have no idea."

"Also, I feel like I have to point out that you destroyed your own life. And you framed me. And you tried to kill me."

"But that's all in the past. I can't hire a private investigator, Dashiell—Dash. If my family suspects that I'm trying to build a defense, they'll clam up. And they certainly won't reveal anything that will give away the truth. And if you're going to find whoever killed my brother, you'll need them to talk to you."

"I haven't said I was going to—"

"And the third reason is because I'm innocent, and I know you won't let an innocent person go to prison while a murderer walks free."

I opened my mouth to say something snarky, but I stopped myself. Instead, I said the only honest thing I could think of: "This feels like a trap."

She laughed, but it was dark and short. "I imagine it does."

"Why don't you tell me what happened to your brother—what you know, I mean—and I'll think about it? I'm not making any promises."

"He disappeared in the summer of 1985," Vivienne said. "June 21. The solstice."

"He—that was over thirty years ago."

"That's right."

"Why are they charging you with murder now?"

"Because his body was found in the slough behind his home." She spoke with a chilling matter-of-factness that reminded me that Vivienne Carver was no stranger to gruesome death. "It had been weighted down and hidden in the water, but something must have given way, because some bones washed ashore a few weeks ago. They identified the body with dental records, and my family was quick to explain to the police that I must have killed him."

"Why?"

"Because they're hoping for a civil suit. They've always wanted to get their hands on my money."

That was...a lot, but I said, "No, I meant why do they say you killed him?"

"Ask them yourself."

The next gust of breeze carried a spray of water against my cheek, and it was cold and bracing. The sun glinted on the saw-toothed waves. When I glanced down the pier, Mr. Li waved and smiled, and somehow, I managed to wave back.

"Vivienne, I'm sorry—I really am. But I don't think I should get involved."

She made an understanding noise. "If you change your mind about letting a killer go unpunished, I'll be happy for any assistance you can provide. I'll have my attorney send you a photograph of Richard and anything else I can think of that might help."

"Still not taking the case," I said.

"Of course not."

If Emily Post had written a chapter on "How to End a Collect Call with Your Attempted Murderess," I hadn't read it. So, I said, "Well, goodbye."

For some reason, that made Vivienne laugh. "Goodbye, Dashiell."

"Just—"

The call disconnected.

"—Dash," I finished.

I leaned against the rail, looking out at the ocean and the hot white disc of the sun. Its light was warm on my face. A salt-damp eddy tickled the hairs on the back of my neck. Behind me, screams of excitement suggested the little girl had finally gotten her kite into the air.

Vivienne Carver was a cold-blooded murderer. She'd tried to kill me. I didn't feel sorry for her. I didn't think she deserved some sort of second chance. Another murder charge wouldn't change the fact that she was going to spend the rest of her life in prison.

But if she was telling the truth, another killer would walk free.

Did it matter? The question had a kind of icy clarity that unbalanced me. Vivienne's brother had been murdered over thirty years ago, and that was a long time. Longer than I'd been alive, as a matter of fact. After all that time, did it matter if the killer was found and brought to justice—assuming such a thing was even possible at this point?

The answer came immediately. Yes, it mattered. It mattered because no matter how that family felt about Vivienne, they were grieving their loss all over again—even if the discovery of his body provided some closure, it would also open old wounds. And it mattered because every death mattered. Every injustice mattered. And because no one should be allowed to take another's life and get away with it.

And I realized, with a cold wave of horror rising in me, that I was going to do it.

Just like Vivienne had known I would.

The Last Picks would be thrilled, of course—for a variety of reasons. Bobby, on the other hand, would probably murder me—if he wasn't too busy playing patty-cake with his latest flavor of the week.

That gave me an idea.

I placed a call on my phone, and Bobby answered on the second ring. A blow dryer cut off. He was getting ready for his date.

"You know how we had that big fight a few months ago?"

"Hi," Bobby said. And then, voice dry, "You'll have to be more specific."

"Bobby!"

The sounds of movement came from the other side. His voice was muffled for the first few words, and I realized he was pulling on a shirt. Was he naked? Nope. I was not going to think about *that*. Scratch that from the record, uh, judge. "I'm in a hurry. What's up?"

"When I, um, did some investigating—"

"Snooping."

"—at the amusement park, and it turned out the killer was still there—"

"And they would have killed you if someone hadn't saved your hide." Bobby's tone was treacherously deadpan.

"Actually, I was doing a great job on my own—"

"I'm hanging up in five seconds."

"You told me that if I was going to do something stupid, I should have told you because you're my friend."

His silence had the quality of a *lot* of teeth-grinding.

"Well," I said in a small voice, "I'm about to do something stupid."

Chapter 3

The drive up the coast wasn't exactly comfortable. The Jeep isn't the smoothest of rides, plus it's surprisingly noisy inside, and there was also the little issue of Bobby's ferocious silence as he rode shotgun.

About every five miles, I said, "Thank you again for coming."

And every five miles, Bobby said nothing.

That kind of thing can make a relatively easy drive feel a lot longer.

Vivienne's attorney had provided addresses for the house where her brother had lived at the time of his disappearance, as well as for Vivienne's father's home. The numbers were only different by a digit, so I figured they were neighbors. The homes were located in a neighborhood outside Astoria. On a normal day—when I wasn't stuck inside the time-warping effects of my best friend's silent anger—the drive would have taken an hour, tops. Today, though, it felt like it took about a month to get halfway there, and trust me: no matter how beautiful the coast is, or the spruce and pine forests, or the restless prism of the ocean, nobody wants to spend a month with Bobby's extremely loud silence.

So, it was a relief when Bobby picked up his phone, scrolled, tapped, scrolled, tapped, and held it to his ear. When he spoke, his voice had his usual crisp, no-nonsense tone. "This is Deputy Mai from the Ridge County Sheriff's Office. I'm calling because—yep, you got it. Thanks." What followed was a one-sided conversation in which Bobby didn't actually have to do a lot of talking. In fact, once he had identified himself again, he mostly listened.

When he put down the phone, he stared out the windshield and said, "A woman walking her dog found the body on June 3."

Spend enough time at the dinner table with my parents, and fun conversation topics like decomp rates come up. I'd done plenty of research of my own, too, and I had an idea of the condition Richard Lundgren's body would have been in. "Yikes."

Bobby nodded. "They identified the body from dental records, like Vivienne told you. And, like she told you, Richard Lundgren went missing thirty-three years ago on June 21, 1985."

"Was that the police department?"

"Yes."

"And they just told you that stuff?"

"They gave me that information because the Ridge County Sheriff's Office has a vested interest in any investigations related to Vivienne Carver."

"Oh."

"And because Sheriff Acosta called them earlier to tell them I'd be calling."

"Uh. Oh." Which meant Bobby had called the sheriff after I'd pitched this little outing to him. "Was she mad?"

"She wasn't happy. For heaven's sake, Dash, Vivienne killed two people. She almost killed you. She framed an innocent woman for murder and let her spend her life in prison. And that's just the stuff we know about. How do you think the sheriff is going to feel when she finds out you're on a mission to prove Vivienne's innocence?"

"I wouldn't say I'm on a mission—"

"The sheriff also told me," Bobby said over me, "that I don't have any legal authority in this investigation. And she told me if we get ourselves in a jam, we're on our own because this isn't my job, and it's not part of the deal she worked out with you."

"And just to be clear—" I braced myself. "—are *you* mad?"

"You're the detective," he said, still staring out the window. "Figure it out."

That was a very *un*-Bobby-like thing to say.

"Bobby, it's not about proving Vivienne's innocence. It's about the fact that if she didn't kill her brother, someone else did—and that person shouldn't be allowed to get away with it. And I know what you're going to say—"

He turned in his seat abruptly and said, "Do you?"

I swallowed. "Uh—"

"What am I going to say, Dash?"

I couldn't bring myself to meet his eyes, so I kept my attention on the road. "You're going to say that the Astoria police can handle it, and if she's innocent, they'll sort it out, and it's none of our business."

"No, that's not what I was going to say."

"Okay. Were you going to say that you understand this kind of thing is important to me, and that justice matters, and this is our chance to do something good?"

"No."

We passed a faded sign of painted plywood advertising a produce stand, but there was no indication where the stand might have once stood or where we were supposed to go. The state highway carried us inland until the ocean was no longer visible. The trees thinned out, and we started to drive between agricultural fields. In one, an aging outbuilding of corrugated metal, with rust-eaten skirting and paint peeling from its roof, stood alone on ground allowed to go fallow. In another, a woman had crawled under what I wanted to call a combine, and she appeared to be venting her frustration with a wrench. Brush grew in patches along the sides of the road—not the ferns I was accustomed to around Hemlock House, but desiccated tangles of blackberry and hawthorn. Startled by something I couldn't see, a sparrow launched itself from one of the blackberry bushes and zipped away.

In what I thought was a moment of particular genius, I said, "Do you want to tell me what you were going to say?"

"Not particularly."

I had to work some spit into my mouth before I could talk, and then—somehow—what came out of my mouth was "Okey-dokey."

That should have been my cue, ladies and gentlemen. That, right there. I should have steered straight for the closest outbuilding, combine, or utility pole and put myself out of my misery. (I assume Bobby would have been thrown clear and escaped without a scratch.)

After a deep breath—or three—Bobby said, "The county medical examiner doesn't have much to work with, but she didn't see any signs of physical trauma."

I wasn't sure how much soft tissue would remain after thirty years in the water, but my guess was not much, which meant that the only place the medical examiner would be able to look for signs of whatever killed Richard Lundgren were his bones. And while bones could provide a lot of evidence—hey, they made a whole TV show about that—people could be killed in all sorts of ways.

"What you're saying," I said, trying to keep my voice light, "is we're not going to luck into an obvious cause of death and an even more obvious and personally identifying weapon and have everything wrapped up by dinner."

"Interesting," Bobby said. "You knew what I was going to say. Again."

"No, that's not what I—" But I stopped myself. "Maybe I should stop talking."

Bobby didn't say anything, but he did make a noise that sounded an awful lot like "Hmm."

In my infinite wisdom, I decided driving the rest of the way in silence was the best course. The fields and pastures gave way to homes. Then neighborhoods began to appear. To my surprise, the GPS didn't take us into Astoria itself but kept us south of the city. The homes here were small frame constructions. I put most of them somewhere between fifty and seventy years old, with slab foundations and—where it hadn't been replaced by vinyl—

aluminum siding. One house needed its roof replaced. Another had a gutter hanging like a dropped jaw. Green algae bloomed on the north side of one little box of a house. The lawns varied—most were cut short, with a kind of ruthless utilitarianism that exposed brown patches and crabgrass. Just to keep things interesting, though, others were overgrown. One homeowner had chosen to go with the "abandoned toys" theme, and their yard was littered with action figures, trikes, and a Batman bicycle. It had the Bat Signal in yellow against the black body and shiny black tassels on the handlebars. I wondered if they made the same model, but for an adult.

Bobby was looking at me. My brain snapped the realization at me, and my face flushed. Because I was still—perpetually—Dashiell Dawson Dane, I blurted the first thing that popped into my head: "I know you're going to think I'm crazy, but those tassels would definitely make that bike go faster."

To my surprise, Bobby let out a breath that was almost a laugh. He rubbed his face, and when he lowered his hands, he looked like Bobby again—as though, until this moment, he'd been wearing a mask that just looked like Bobby. It was disorienting because it hadn't been until now that I'd realized the difference. When he spoke, his voice was Bobby's voice. "There's no way they'd make the bike go faster."

"Oh, they totally would. They're awesome."

"How would that make the bike faster?"

"It's science, Bobby. Try to keep up."

For a heartbeat, that goofy smile flickered on his face. And then he said, "I'm sorry I've been short with you. Kiefer—"

But he stopped.

Kiefer what, I wanted to know. Kiefer yelled at you? Kiefer picked a fight? Kiefer got angry because you're a deputy and sometimes your job comes first? (Echoes of West.) And then another option sent a dark little thrill through me: Kiefer was furious because you chose to spend time with me over the date you'd planned with him. I wasn't sure I liked what that feeling said about me, but it was there, and I couldn't deny it.

Bobby didn't look like he was going to finish that thought, so I said, "Bobby, I'm sorry."

He shook his head.

"No, I am. I shouldn't have asked—it's just, you told me you wanted me to tell you—"

"I do want you to tell me." The words were firm. "I don't want you doing anything risky without telling me."

"But I should have thought about your date."

"Yeah, well." Bobby ran his hand along the seat belt, pulling it away from his chest and letting it fall back into place.

"I forgot."

He nodded.

"Next time," I said, "just remind me. We could have gone tomorrow."

A smile tilted across his face. "Really? You would have waited until I got off work tomorrow evening?"

"Uh...yes?"

"That's what I thought."

"Okay, I'm not sorry anymore because that was super rude. I take back my sorry. If anything, I'm reverse sorry."

"What does that mean?" Bobby asked drily. "You're glad you ruined my date?"

I opened my mouth and nothing came out.

Would *yes* be such a terrible thing to say?

Instead, though, I gave Bobby a sheepish smile. And he smiled back. And we were both smiling. I think maybe we even laughed a little. Like we both knew it was a joke. Like we both knew we were supposed to pretend it was a joke.

Remember how earlier I had that stroke of genius about driving into a utility pole?

I should have stuck with the plan.

Maybe Bobby was trying to come up with a similar plan to get out of this mess because his voice took on its usual business-like briskness, and he said, "So, how does an amateur sleuth solve a thirty-year-old mystery?"

"That question feels like a trap." But Bobby only looked at me, and after a moment, I said, "You mean in a book?"

The rumble of the Jeep's engine filled the silence between us.

"Well," I said, "in a *book*, a cold case—which I guess is what this is—usually isn't all too different from a regular investigation. Unless you're writing a police procedural or about a forensic scientist, your protagonist probably won't have access to approaches that involve DNA evidence or gas chromatography-mass spectrometry or carbon dating. Or, heck, even an autopsy."

"So, what do they do?"

"Well, they talk to people. They ask questions."

"This is starting to sound familiar."

"I told you it was pretty much the same," I said with a grin. "Usually, the detective is trying to find something that was overlooked or concealed when the mystery was first investigated. They're looking for new information, or lies, or a mistaken assumption—anything that will help establish means, motive, and opportunity."

"That seems incredibly unrealistic. Wouldn't people have forgotten the details after all those years? Or told the police in the first place?"

"Sure. But people also lie for all sorts of reasons, and sometimes, later on, the reasons for those lies become less important. Or they feel pressured to finally tell the truth. Or someone the police never talked to turns up. I mean, we're talking about books, Bobby. Something convenient always happens. And if it's not talking to people, the detective might do archival research or read someone's journal. There's even a whole branch of mystery novels about people who solve murders with genealogy."

Bobby said something *very* un-Bobby-like under his breath.

I burst out laughing.

"If this involves you getting an Ancestry.com subscription," Bobby said, "I'll buy you dinner."

"It's a date."

That did it again. The good humor that had been defrosting the ice between us vanished, and we drove the rest of the distance in an uncomfortable silence.

Fortunately, it wasn't long before the GPS announced that our destination was on the left. The address belonging to Richard Lundgren—or, better said, where Richard had been living when he'd disappeared—was a little square house that could only by the loosest stretch of the imagination be called a bungalow. Like the rest of the neighborhood, it fell into the category of tract housing that had clearly been designed for working-class families. The Lundgren home looked clean and well-maintained, with that severe attention to detail that suggested high standards but without any sense of adornment. A couple of generations ago, when these houses had been going up, the men and women who lived here would have worked in Astoria's timber and fishing industries. Those industries had shrunk over the years, though. Some of the people here might still work the line at a fishery, or they might crew a fishing boat, but for the rest, hard times had come to stay.

The address that belonged to Vivienne's father, Arlen Lundgren, was next door. It looked like a twin to Richard's, which made sense considering the tract-housing style of the neighborhood, and it appeared to be similarly well kept. The only difference was that someone had hung hideous curtains in Arlen's windows—some sort of eye-wrenching print of mauve-colored roses—and a few bare, brittle rosebushes huddled next to the stoop. There was no sign that anyone was home at either residence; with the curtains closed, the houses looked still and lifeless.

I unlocked my phone and examined the photo that Vivienne's lawyer had sent me. It had the saturated colors that I associated with quick, cheap photos from another era, and it showed a close-up of a young man. He had a kind of attractiveness that was a combination of strong features and youth that didn't quite translate into handsomeness—a high brow, prominent nose, and heavy jaw that, combined with hair the color of wheat, gave him a distinctly Norse look. Even in the close-up, it was easy to tell that he was well built and vital. A thousand years ago, he would have made one heck of a Viking. He was pushing one hand through his hair, as though the photo were a candid one, and he'd been caught unaware, and on that wrist he wore a bracelet that consisted of a fine gold chain and what I guessed was a small saint medallion.

"He doesn't look like he'd be easy to overpower," Bobby said.

I shook my head.

"We can rule out a gun or a blow to the head," Bobby continued. "The medical examiner would have seen some kind of evidence if that's how it happened."

"Which leaves some kind of drug to incapacitate him." I sighed. "And in books, poison is a woman's weapon."

"Good thing this isn't a book," Bobby said with that slanting smile again.

I got out of the Jeep, but instead of heading to the front door of the house that had belonged, at one point, to Richard Lundgren, I headed toward the backyard. A few windows were set into the side of the house, and these were curtained as well. The back of the house had a few more, and finally I got a glimpse of bare, dark glass—no curtains, but I couldn't make out anything inside the house without walking up and pressing my nose to the window, which I wasn't quite ready to do. A rusting gas grill on wheels, plastic patio furniture that looked brittle and washed out from UV exposure, and a few planters that held nothing but weeds were the only suggestion that someone used this space.

As with the front of the house, the landscaping—if you could call it that—was really nothing more than mercilessly short grass.

Bobby stood, hands on hips, and looked out at the slough. I followed his gaze. The water began maybe forty yards from the patio, with rushes and sedge bristling at the waterline. A thin scum of algae covered the water, which appeared to be stagnant—if the water was flowing or had a current, I couldn't tell. It wasn't a wide body of water, maybe another thirty or forty yards, and I doubted it was deep. I guess it had been deep enough, I thought with a sick feeling. But the slough *was* long. I couldn't see the end of it in either direction. A broken length of barricade tape floated on the water, which I took to mean that the local police were no longer even pretending to try to preserve the scene.

"Maybe someone killed him somewhere else and brought him up here in a kayak," I said, taking another, longer look up the slough.

Bobby shook his head. "Too complicated." He swung his gaze back to the house.

I knew what he was thinking. "Forty yards isn't nothing, but someone could have dragged him from the house to the slough. Even a much smaller woman."

Bobby nodded, but he said, "But she would have been exposed the whole time. If anyone had looked out the window, they would have seen her."

We both turned to consider the house next door. A man stood there, and he was holding a shotgun. My first, confused thought was: How long has he been there? I hadn't heard him, and to judge by Bobby's sudden stillness, neither had he. Then my brain began to take in the details of his appearance. He was old—not just older, but *old*, in his eighties, maybe even older. He had a surprising amount of white hair left, and the color of it made me think of Ivory soap. He wore a brown, waffle-weave bathrobe, and he had on some kind of rubber clogs that looked like knock-off Crocs. Gun, my brain told me again. I tried to make sense of how he'd gotten the drop on us—he couldn't have come out of the house, or we would have heard the ancient storm door. But there was a detached garage next to the house, as well as a freestanding building that I took to be a workshop or a storage shed, and he could have come from either of those. It was hard to focus, though; my brain kept saying, Gun.

The man said, "Who the fudge are you?"

(He didn't say fudge.)

And then he brought the gun up toward us.

Chapter 4

Staring at the shotgun pointed my direction, I made a snap decision: I was going to tackle Bobby.

It wasn't a rational thought. It wasn't a logical conclusion. It's hard to even call it a plan, since it was something that seemed to happen at the cellular level. Someone was aiming a weapon at us, and my body tensed, seemingly of its own accord, as I readied myself. There wasn't any sort of intermediate process.

"Sir—" Deputy Bobby said, in his best deputy voice.

"Daddy!"

The storm door clattered open, and a woman lowered herself down the steps in a flustered hustle that was impeded by the fact that she had to hold on to the rail with both hands and take each step one at a time. My first impression was of middle-aged dumpiness—the short, frizzy hair that had been fried blond; the extra weight; the varicose veins. But then I realized that wasn't quite right, because even though middle age came to everyone, this woman had overlaid hers with a veneer of gas station chic. Instead of a dressing gown or a robe, she wore a plasticky kimono with a dragon on its back. Her nails were a fire-engine red, visible even at a distance. And when the breeze shifted, the fetor of the slough was replaced by something I could only imagine she called *scent*.

"Daddy," she said again, as she lowered herself to the patio behind the house next door. "Put that down! You're going to get someone killed!"

The old man didn't even look at her.

"Put it away!" She pushed on the shotgun's barrel until it lowered, and then she planted herself in front of him, balled up her fists, and set them on her hips. "What in the world's gotten into you?" But she didn't wait for a reply. She turned around. Apparently we didn't deserve the fists-on-hips treatment, because one of her hands drifted up to clutch the kimono shut at the neck, while the other patted the air around her hair (not the hair itself, I was careful to note, which I was beginning to suspect was *supposed* to look that way). "I'm sorry. Daddy's always been protective of his little girl."

Then she giggled.

Bobby, bless his heart, was staring.

"She's batting her eyelashes at you," I whispered.

"You two must have had the fright of your lives." The saccharine tone switched when she snapped, "Go back inside, Daddy!"

The old man gave us another long, lingering look before going inside. With the threat of imminent death removed, I was starting to think a little more clearly, and I did some mental math. It was possible—heck, it was likely—that this man was Vivienne's father. It was difficult to imagine Vivienne having a father—or being a child, for that matter. But what was even more difficult was imagining that this woman was—what? Vivienne's sister?

Whoever she was, she was all sugar again, swishing toward us in her kimono. "Are you all right? Honey, you look like you need to sit down."

That last bit was directed toward Bobby, who was *still* staring. That surprised me a bit; Bobby was, under normal circumstances, unflappable. I'd once seen Mr. Cheek (owner of Fog Belt Ladies Wear, and a fervent admirer of Deputy Mai) lock himself in a dressing room so that Bobby would have to rescue him, only to jump into Bobby's arms once Bobby got the door open. And Bobby had handled it like a champ (although he'd been less patient when Mr. Cheek had tried to unbutton his shirt). Right now, though, Bobby seemed to be having trouble processing what was going on, and it took me a moment to realize that he was trying to decide if he should act like a deputy.

I decided to take pity on him. "I'm sorry about coming back here unannounced. We should have knocked."

"What? Oh, you mean Daddy. He's always like that; it wouldn't matter if you knocked." She had gotten close enough now that she reached up and pressed the back of her hand to Bobby's forehead. "You're like ice! I think you're going into shock."

Bobby did not look like he was going into shock. Bobby looked like he might be going into deputy mode, and like he was about to begin dispatching all problems with extreme professionalism.

"We didn't get a chance to introduce ourselves," I said before the voice of the law could ruin everything. "I'm Dash Dane, and this is Bobby—"

"Oh my Gawd!" (You could hear the w.) "I thought I recognized you! Oh my Gawd! Oh my Gawd! I'm Candy Yamamoto. Candace, but I go by Candy. Candy Lundgren." As though waiting for me to connect the dots, she rolled her eyes at Bobby and added, "Vivienne's sister."

I mean, okay. Technically anything was possible. And the longer I looked at her, the more I could detect a family resemblance—in the chin, more than anywhere else. If somebody bleached the dickens out of Vivienne's hair and then plugged her into a light socket, maybe it would have been easier to match them up. But she certainly didn't act like someone whose brother's body had just been discovered. And even though I'd been expecting something like this—even though I'd already guessed, or half-guessed, that she was Vivienne's sister—it was one thing to float a hypothesis, and another to have it confirmed.

Because I honestly couldn't imagine someone more different from the Vivienne Carver I knew. Vivienne was all polish, all class. Vivienne was a razor-sharp mind. She was like Dr. Moriarty in Jackie O's body. (Okay, that was *definitely* a book I was going to have to write.) And Candy Yamamoto, née Lundgren, was…not.

I felt bad as soon as I thought it. It was unkind, first of all. And it was grounded in nothing but a first impression. I didn't know Candy. I didn't know anything about her at all.

But as she pressed Bobby's hands between her own (and, in the process, managed to bring his hand to her, uh, bosom), I had the feeling that, sometimes, first impressions were right on the money.

"I can't believe you're here," she said. "I saw you on the news. You're *much* cuter in person."

"Um, thank you?"

"You've got to tell them to shoot you from your left, honey. Your left is your good side. No, wait, let me see. Well, maybe it's your right. I don't know!" This seemed to titillate her to no end—she burst out into fresh giggles.

"It's definitely his right," Bobby said.

Hands on her hips, she considered Bobby now. "And *you*," she said, "don't have a bad side."

"Thank you," Bobby said.

"Oh, you know what you need?" She patted herself down. "You need a tattoo! Give you a bit of an edge. I've got a butterfly—if you're good, I'll show you—and my friend owns the Skin Art Collective, that's where we all hang out—dang it, I *know* I have one of his cards." And if my head wasn't about to explode already from a sixty-something woman spouting phrases like *that's where we all hang out*, she went and topped it by giving Bobby a coquettish look and adding, "He's not my boyfriend, if that's what you're wondering."

And Bobby said, "How do you know I don't have a tattoo already?"

That was it. The end. My head officially exploded.

Candy, who was now somehow holding Bobby's hand again, gave him a playful swat. "Oh you!"

"Yes," I somehow managed to say. "Oh you."

I know nobody's going to believe me. I know that I'm going to sound like I'm making things up. I know it's flat-out crazy. But even though I can't prove it, I swear to God, in that moment, staring back at me with his typical impassive expression, Bobby winked at me.

"But what are you doing here?" Candy asked.

"It's a long story—" I began.

"We heard about your brother," Bobby said.

Which, to be fair, could have been taken any number of ways.

Candy chose to take it one particular way. Her eyes widened, and her expression quickened with what I wanted to call restrained jubilation. She looked like someone trying not to smile at a funeral. "You're sleuthing!"

"I'd call it investigating—" I tried.

But Candy spoke over me. "You've got to come inside so I can tell you *everything*."

And without missing a beat, she looped her arm through Bobby's and towed him toward the house. Bobby cast a backward glance at me, and I wanted to call *his* expression restrained you're-going-to-pay-for-this.

Candy led us into the kitchen, which was, thankfully, free of any sign of her shotgun-toting father. It was a small, white space, and the only color came from the mauve-colored roses on the curtains and a Formica table that had to be at least fifty years old and was the same shade of green as a stick of chewing gum. Frilly tea towels hung from the oven door's handle. A polyester mat on the table supported a vase of dusty plastic flowers. A cross-stitch sampler hung above the sink with the words TRUST IN THE LORD WITH ALL YOUR HEART. It might have been kitsch in the right hands, but instead, it felt like someone had died, and they hadn't cleaned out the house yet. The dirty dishes in the sink, and their sour smell, were part of that.

"Sit down, sit down," Candy said, waving at the Formica table and the matching chrome-legged chairs. "Let me get you something to drink."

"We're all right," Bobby said.

"You have to have something to drink. I can make you coffee."

She bent to inspect a lower cabinet, which made the kimono do problematic things.

"We're really fine," I said. "And we don't want to take up too much of your time."

Candy fixed her gaze on me. "I was being polite."

"We'll have coffee," Bobby said.

She didn't actually sniff or shake a finger at me, but her message of disapproval came through loud and clear.

It wasn't until we were all seated around the table with cups of truly subpar Folger's that Candy said, "You're here to prove Vivienne killed him, aren't you? Mind if I smoke?"

"Actually—" I began.

But instead of a cigarette, she took out a vape pen and drew hard on it. The resulting vapor, which smelled like, well, candy, immediately took up residence in my skull in the form of a newborn headache.

"Why do you think we're here to prove Vivienne killed your brother?" Bobby asked.

"Because she *killed* him." Candy's gaze moved to me. "And because he already proved she killed all those other people."

"Could you explain that?" I asked. "It's still not clear to me why anyone thinks Vivienne had anything to do with this."

Candy took another puff of the vape and said, "I told the police all this."

"I know, but it'd be helpful to hear it again."

"They thought it was great stuff. They wrote it all down."

"Uh." Genius struck, and I took out my phone. "I hope I have your permission to record this session."

She rolled her eyes and nodded, and I got the sense that Candy Yamamoto was wondering how a bozo like me had managed to catch Vivienne in the first place.

After I'd started recording, I said, "Could you explain this to us the way you explained it to the police?"

Candy sprang into action. "The first thing you've got to understand is that nobody really knows Viv. I mean, everybody thinks they do. They see this big-name author lady, and they see her in her fancy dresses and with her hair done and those fake nails, and they figure that's who she is. But they don't know the real Viv. Everybody falls for the act, you know?"

I almost—but not quite—said, *Not* everybody.

"See, Viv's only ever cared about one thing: herself. As long as she's been alive, she's been focused on taking care of number one, and she never cared who got hurt in the process." She played with the vape. "Look at Neil."

"Who's Neil?" Bobby asked.

Bobby got a dose of Candy's look too before she said, "Neil Carver. Her *ex*-husband."

I mean, part of me had understood that, at some point, Vivienne had been married—she'd been Mrs. Vivienne Carver, after all. But I'd always assumed that Mr. Carver had gone wherever husbands who were inconvenient to the plot go. (Heaven, presumably?)

"Neil's just the sweetest man on two legs," Candy continued, "and Viv couldn't even hang on to him. It's because she's so cold. Some girls are like that, you know? They don't know how to have fun." At that point, Bobby got a very different kind of look from Candy, and she took a lot of time uncrossing her legs and crossing them again. "It's a shame, too, because Neil's a catch, too. He and Dad still go fishing. Can you believe that?"

"You still see Mr. Carver?" I said.

"Yeah, of course." And then, in a tone meant to suggest it was no big deal, she added, "He takes me to lunch, too. I think that's pretty sweet, don't you?"

I thought about how I'd feel if Hugo still wanted to go hunting with my dad or take my mom out to lunch. The politest phrase was probably *blow a gasket*.

"Very sweet," I said. "Did he—"

"He could have done *much* better for himself," Candy said. "He was *very* popular in high school, and nobody can figure out why he stuck with Viv."

"So, they were—" I tried.

"It's because he and Richard were best friends, of course," Candy said over me. "And Neil's such a sweetheart. Once he realized what a cold fish Viv was, he was in too deep. He stuck it out as long as he could, I guess."

"Neil and Richard were best friends?" Bobby asked.

"They were all friends, the four of them, ever since they were in high school. Richard and Jane, and Neil and Viv. They were going together the whole time. They even wanted to get married on the same day, only Jane got cold feet, and that's why Richard and Jane got married later." Candy took another puff, and the sickly sweet vapor rolled over me. "Don't get me started on *her*," she said, which was apparently preamble for, well, getting started. "Jane never knows when she has a good thing. She and Richard were *always* fighting. I mean, I don't think that's right, do you? It's the woman's job to make her husband happy." She leaned forward and laid her hand over Bobby's. Red nails scratched lightly at his knuckles. "Don't you think?"

Bobby pulled his hand away—politely—and said, "So, Jane is Richard's widow?"

This time, annoyance flickered in Candy's expression. "That's right." And then, as though Bobby had somehow missed something obvious, she added, "I'm divorced, you know. *He* left *me*."

Somehow—barely—I managed to turn my laugh into a cough.

Bobby's sneaker connected with my ankle, and my cough turned into a yelp. His voice was as untroubled as a baby's bathwater (is that an expression?) when he said, "You mentioned arguments. Do you know what Richard and Jane were fighting about?"

"Sex. It's always sex. Or money, I guess, but they didn't have to worry about that. Richard had a good job at the cannery."

As any number of mystery novels or true crime TV shows (hello, *Dateline*) will tell you, a good job and a healthy income have never been obstacles to arguments about money. But I decided to follow up on Candy's obvious bait. "Was Richard having an affair?"

"What? God, no. Richard never even *looked* at another woman. He loved Jane. It was Jane. She was having an affair."

The whisper of a footfall made me glance at the hall that led off from the kitchen, but I couldn't see anyone. I hadn't imagined the sound, though, and when I caught Bobby's eye, I could tell he'd heard it too.

"Do you know that for a fact?" Bobby asked.

"Of course."

"Who was Jane having an affair with?"

Candy opened her mouth to fire off the answer. Then color rushed into her cheeks, and she faltered. "I don't know. Not exactly. But she *was*."

"That sounds like a motive," I said.

"God, no," Candy said. "She never would have hurt Richard. Besides, she wasn't even home that night. See, they had a big fight, and she left." As Candy spoke, her tone changed—the gossipy thrill became more subdued, and her account began to sound formulaic. Either rehearsed, I thought, or memorized. "When she came home the next day, Richard was gone. The money, too."

"The money?" Bobby asked.

"They always kept some money in the house. A few thousand dollars, you know. Richard said it was for emergencies. Anyway, the money was gone. So, Jane came over here—"

"She checked the money first?" I asked. "Before coming over here?"

The question interrupted Candy's flow, and she seemed off balance for a moment before saying, "I don't know." She picked up the thread before I could interrupt again. "She came over here, but none of us had seen him—"

"Were you home that night?" I asked.

"Daddy was taking care of Mommy. She was super sick by then, so by the time she fell asleep, he was exhausted."

"Right, but were *you* home?"

"I just said none of us had seen him!"

It was the first time her annoyance had bled through the story, and the bright edge of it made me sit up a little straighter. Something at the back of my head stirred, and I studied Candy more closely.

Bobby seemed to be considering her more carefully too. "And what happened then?"

The rote nature of Candy's answers changed again, and what sounded like genuine emotion filtered into the words. "It was horrible. Nobody knew what had happened. He was gone, that's all. His friends didn't know where he was. We called the police, and they weren't any help. They thought he'd run away and taken the money with him. By the time they really started looking, we all knew it was too late. They finally said it might have been a robbery. Might." She laughed, and the sound had an old, jaded quality that was the first honest thing I thought I'd heard from her. "They weren't wrong about that."

"What do you mean?" I asked.

"Viv," she said, and her tone suggested that—to borrow Fox's phrase—my cheese done slid off my cracker. "I mean, she wanted to move to Portland. That's all she'd talk about, how she had to get away from here. But Daddy wouldn't give her any money, and she'd already divorced Neil, and she and Richard were at it like cats and dogs all the time."

"Vivienne and Richard fought a lot?"

"And then one day Richard's gone, and the money's gone, and a couple of weeks later, Viv's gone too. Took herself off to Portland. Where'd she get that money from, that's what I wanted to know at the time. Guess we know now."

I tried to wrap my head around that, but Bobby was the one who spoke first. "You think Vivienne killed Richard and took his money because he wouldn't give her enough to move to Portland?"

Candy stared at the vape pen as though she'd forgotten what it was. And then she said, "You know what she did with all that money she made? All those books? The TV show, all of it?" It was a rhetorical question because Candy answered it herself. "She spent it on herself. All of it. She never sent a dime back. You could call her up and tell her you didn't have two nickels to rub together, and she wouldn't give you a cent. She changed her number—did you know that? So we couldn't bother her. Oh, sure, when Daddy got sick—"

Heavy footsteps came from the hall. Candy's father appeared in the opening, his face dark. On my second look at him, I took in the man's big frame. He was tall, and at some point in his life, he had been strong, but now that strength had wasted away, and he had that too-thin look some men age into. "All right, that's enough. Get out of my house."

Bobby only said, "Hello, sir. Who are you?"

"I'm the son of a gun—" (My words, not his.) "—who owns this house, and I want you out. Right now."

"That would make you Arlen Lundgren, then?"

"Daddy," Candy said, "this is Dash Dane."

"I know who he is," Arlen said, "and I want him out of here."

"Mr. Lundgren—" I tried.

"They want to talk to us about Richard," Candy said.

"Talk?" Arlen said. "Nobody wants to talk to you. If men wanted to sit around all day listening to you yap, you'd still have a husband, and I'd have some gosh darn peace and quiet."

(Again, I'm paraphrasing.)

Tears rushed into Candy's eyes, and her doughy cheeks filled with color. "I can talk to whoever I want. Go back to your room—"

"This is my house," Arlen shouted and slapped the wall. The crack of the blow rang out in the tiny house, and Candy jumped out of her chair. She raced past Arlen, and a moment later, a door slammed shut. Then Arlen turned his gaze on me and Bobby.

"Mr. Lundgren," I said, "Vivienne asked us to help—"

"That woman hasn't been part of this family for thirty years. She's no daughter of mine, and I don't care what she wants or how much she told you she'd pay you."

"No," I said, "that's not—"

"You get out of here. And don't come back."

At a nod from Bobby, I got to my feet. We'd barely made it out the door when he slammed it behind us, and as the crash faded, I thought I could hear Candy crying in the distance.

Bobby and I made our way around front, and we got in the Jeep. I started it up. And then I said, "That could have gone better."

"Drive to the end of the street," Bobby said.

"What?"

"Drive to the end of the street," Bobby said again. "And park where he won't be able to see us."

"Wait, what—"

"I don't know," Bobby said. "Let's see."

I drove to the end of the street, turned around, and parked at the curb. The houses here all had their curtains pulled, and while I was sure that some nosy neighbor would notice us—or had already noticed us—it wasn't like we were running a professional stakeout. This was more of the bargain bin variety—

The front door to Arlen Lundgren's house flew open, and Candy lurched outside. She looked like a mess—even from a distance, I could tell she was crying, and although she'd changed into jeans and some sort of sparkly top, her clothes looked like they'd been thrown on. She was carrying a purse that could have doubled as a shipping container, as well as several other plastic shopping bags that—I guessed—contained whatever she could grab close at hand. One of them appeared to hold a lamp.

Arlen appeared in the doorway a moment later, steadying himself with one hand on the jamb, and he said something. Candy whirled around and screamed back at him. She was loud enough that I might have been able to make out the words, but they were distorted by her rage. Arlen snapped something back at her, but before she could reply, he went back inside and slammed the door. Candy screamed at him again. Nobody came out to check on them, and I had the feeling this wasn't anything new. It had all the pathetic weariness of two people playing parts they'd played for years—parts they should have aged out of a long time ago.

Candy stumbled around the side of the house, in the direction of the garage and workshop I'd noticed when we'd been, uh, exploring. I waited, but a car didn't appear. After a few minutes, Bobby nodded, and I started the Jeep again.

We were halfway to the Lundgren house when a truck turned onto the street ahead of us. It barreled down the street, well above the speed limit, and then turned sharply into the Lundgrens' driveway. I waffled for a moment between stopping the Jeep or continuing, but I decided to continue. Stopping would have looked even more suspicious. We passed the truck as the driver got out, and he stopped, hand on top of the cab, and looked over at us.

He had a dark, refined complexion that was too different from the Lundgrens' Scandinavian coloring for him to be a blood relation: dark hair that was thinning on top, and dark eyes. A pleasant-looking guy who wasn't exactly handsome but probably didn't give himself grief when he looked in the mirror. A bracelet with what I was fairly sure was a small saint medallion glittered on his wrist in the stark June sunlight, and I thought I remembered seeing it before. Then he threw the door shut and headed toward the garage. On the back of the truck, a bumper sticker said, WE AIN'T QUAINT.

I pulled to the curb again to watch.

"Someone called him," Bobby said.

I nodded. "Want to bet that's Neil Carver?"

"And he got here fast."

"Did you see the bracelet?"

Bobby glanced over at me.

I thought about being mature. I thought about acting like an adult. Instead, in my too-cool voice, I said, "You know, little gold thing on his wrist."

"I know what a bracelet is."

"Oh. Okay." I waited just long enough before adding, "Then you noticed it looks a lot like the one Richard Lundgren's wearing in the picture Vivienne gave us."

Bobby's face doesn't usually give a lot away.

But it was enough to make me grin.

Before I could follow up on that mixture of exasperation and what I wanted to call pique, movement behind us drew my attention. A woman stood on the stoop of the house next to Arlen Lundgren's—the house where Richard Lundgren had been living when he'd been killed. She was White, and she was tall and wiry, with her long gray hair in a braid that fell almost to her waist. She was looking at the truck, taking nervous steps back and forth as though unsure of what to do.

The decision was taken out of her hands when the man I suspected was Neil Carver came down the drive again. He looked once in our direction, and there's no way he could have missed the Jeep, but he didn't storm down the street to confront us. Instead, he headed toward the house that had belonged to Richard Lundgren. The woman said something to Neil, and he shook his head and made a shooing gesture and followed her inside. He shut the door behind them without giving us another glance.

"What in the world is going on?" I asked.

Bobby shook his head, but his gaze stayed fixed on the house. "No clue. But if we're still making bets, how much would you wager that woman is Richard Lundgren's widow?"

Chapter 5

The Otter Slide was busy that night. Under the green-and-gold pendants, the booths were full, and every table had bodies crammed around it. More people packed the bar—along with pretty much every other square inch of floor space.

For the most part, those people were locals—the Otter Slide didn't have the quaint, seaside-dollhouse aesthetic that so many tourists were looking for. But some of these people were out-of-towners, if only because the Otter Slide was the closest thing to a gay bar in Hastings Rock. Voices competed with the music (Seely, the bar's owner, had declared tonight to be country night, and "Jolene" was playing at full volume over the bar's speakers), and men and women laughed and shouted and called out drink orders and, in one case, screamed (a busty young lady who had gotten particularly excited over her latest round at the pinball machine). The air smelled like the nectar of the gods (marinara sauce, fried cheese, and of course, Seely's hamburgers, which somehow the cook managed to do just perfectly, smashed thin on the griddle, with extra crispy edges), and I was enjoying a surprisingly delicious summer highball—some sort of variation with a hint of peach, courtesy of Bobby.

Bobby was also the reason we had managed to snag a booth—he'd been watching the other patrons like a hawk, which was one of his God-given talents, and as soon as a group of them got up, Bobby swooped in. It was a tight fit, with Bobby and Fox and me on one side, and Keme, Millie, and Indira on the other.

But, if I was being honest, Keme didn't look like the close quarters were bothering him too much.

"They're DEFINITELY hiding something," Millie announced.

I managed not to roll my eyes, but only because Keme was giving me a death ray-level warning look. "Right, of course they're hiding something. The question is: what?"

Millie perked right up. She was practically vibrating with excitement. "A SECRET!"

The tourists in the next booth turned around. A guy with a wispy attempt at a mustache stared, his mouth hanging open.

I gave the group a little wave, and slowly, they turned back to their drinks.

That was when Keme kicked me.

"Ow! What did *I* do?"

But he just scowled at me.

"It's all very strange," Fox said as though nothing had happened. "And the case against Vivienne certainly seems thin. Any defense lawyer worth their salt should be able to create reasonable doubt. I mean, Richard's relationship with his wife should be enough all on its own—the ongoing arguments, their fight the night of the murder, the fact that she was having an affair."

"Was she having the affair with Neil?" Indira asked.

I blinked. "That possibility hadn't occurred to me."

"Maybe that's why they're married," Millie said.

I blinked again. In the background, Dolly was begging Jolene not to steal her man. "Neil and—what's her name? Jane?"

Millie nodded.

"They're not married," I said. "Neil and Vivienne were married, but they got divorced. And Richard and Jane were married, but Richard died."

"No, Neil and Jane are married NOW." She held up her phone. "They're old, so they put everything on Facebook."

I snatched the phone from her—which, I noted in my peripheral vision, earned me another dark look from Keme—and studied the screen. It was Neil Carver's Facebook page, and sure enough, it showed that he'd married Jane Lundgren Carver in 1990.

"Five years after Richard disappeared," I said.

"After he died," Bobby said. He frowned. "That's strange."

Indira frowned. "I'm not sure it is. After all, Candy told you that the four of them were all close in high school. Vivienne had moved away. Richard was gone. I don't think it's all that unusual for two people who were already close and both dealing with different kinds of loss to find comfort in each other."

Millie shot up in her seat again. "OR THEY KILLED HIM TOGETHER!"

"Usually, we try not to sound so gleeful," I muttered with another apologetic wave for the people in the next booth. Wispy Mustache Guy had spilled his drink on himself.

"That certainly seems like a possibility," Fox said, "but why? I mean, if they were having an affair and wanted to be together, Jane could have divorced Richard and married Neil. It was the 1980s, not the 1880s."

"An argument," I said. "Candy told us Richard and Jane were fighting constantly. They had a fight the night Richard disappeared. Jane left the house that night, according to Candy, but maybe when she came back, the fight picked up again and got out of hand."

Keme said, "Or *he* did it."

"That's a good point," Indira said. "It's equally likely that Richard argued with Neil about the affair. Like you said, Dash, things might have escalated. He certainly seems to have stepped into Richard's life—the jewelry, the house, the wife."

"Except there doesn't seem to be any evidence of a physical altercation," Bobby said. "Remember? The medical examiner didn't find anything."

Waving the words away, Fox said, "She poisoned him. A little antifreeze in his coffee every morning."

"Aren't we forgetting someone?" Bobby waited, and when no one spoke, he said, "We've already got a suspect we know is guilty of multiple homicides. I'm not saying that automatically makes her guilty, but she's got to be a consideration."

I shrugged. "I know, but I can't figure out why Vivienne would ask me to investigate if she's the one who killed Richard. I mean, why not leave it alone? Or let the police investigate and try to build a case? It's not like it's going to matter one way or another, with the sentences she's already facing."

"I think it *does* matter, though," Indira said. "I'm not saying it means Vivienne's innocent, but Vivienne cared—cares—deeply about her appearance. I don't think she was exaggerating when she said she didn't want to be known as a kin slayer."

"Plus, she might want revenge," Millie said. "Oh, Dash, maybe she wants revenge on you too, and THIS IS PART OF THE PLAN!"

"Uh, thanks, Millie. I hadn't considered that terrifying possibility yet."

Keme pushed his hair behind his ears and said, "What about the dad?"

Bobby and I looked at each other.

"That lady, the sister, she told you the dad got sick," Keme said. "Maybe he needed the money."

"I think that was later," I said slowly. "Candy was talking about Vivienne by that point, about how she'd never share her money. But you might be on to something. He definitely didn't like that we were looking at the slough. And he was eavesdropping on the conversation."

Bobby made a face. "I should have thought of that. It wasn't until Candy brought him up in the conversation that he interrupted, and then he couldn't get us out of there fast enough."

"You know who I think did it?" Millie said. She waited, and I could tell she was working up to something, but even so, I wasn't prepared for the sheer magnitude of: "CANDY!"

In the next booth, a glass shattered. (Kidding.)

"They're sisters, right?" Millie said. "And it sounds like Candy is SUPER jealous of Vivienne, like, her success and everything. AND—" She even held up a finger. "—she was eager to insert herself in the investigation so she could tell you bad stuff about everyone else, which is what some killers do because they want attention. I saw that on TV when Fox made me watch that show with all the widows who were killing each other."

"I have no idea what that was," Fox said, "but I want to watch it again."

I opened my mouth, but before I could speak, Millie said, "AND Candy had opportunity, in terms of the murder. She lived right next door to Richard, and she was home the night he disappeared. And Dash, you always say that if we can establish opportunity, then we consider the person a suspect and look for motive."

"I do?" I asked.

"There was definitely something off about her," Bobby said.

"The kimono," I said.

"She has a lot of resentment—"

"The nail polish."

"—and she was quick to blame Vivienne—"

"Oh, and she fell instantly in love with Bobby. So, zero gaydar."

"—but her explanation for why she believes it was Vivienne is pretty weak." Bobby turned in his seat. "Do you want to go over that last part again?"

I grinned and shook my head.

"She fell in love with you?" Millie actually clasped her hands. "That's so sweet!"

"Bobby doesn't show up on gaydar," Fox said. "He's not even a blip. Oh, except when I saw him snogging that little powderpuff on the boardwalk the other day. Was that Kiefer?"

"No," Bobby said, and I thought a little color came into his cheeks, "and—"

"It's the way he walks," Keme said.

"Oh my God," Millie said. "It IS the way he walks. AND HIS HAIR."

"His hair—" I tried.

At the same time, Bobby said, "My hair—"

"And his jeans," Fox said. "Marvelous hind end, but sometimes it's like a pair of bowling balls swimming around in a denim sack."

"What is happening?" Bobby said, mostly to himself.

"Just let it wash over you," I said. "They wear themselves out eventually." In a louder voice—to our alleged friends—I said, "Bobby shows up just fine on gaydar, thank you very much. And for your information, it's fine for some gay guys, like us, to present as more traditionally masculine."

Silence.

A single, nervously high giggle escaped Millie before she clamped a hand over her mouth.

Keme pulled up his hood and appeared to die quietly of secondhand embarrassment.

Fox fixed their gaze in the middle distance.

But worst of all was Indira, who stretched across the table to PAT MY HAND.

And Bobby looked like he was dedicating all his considerable skill to keeping his face expressionless.

"Are you guys kidding me?" I asked.

"Don't answer that," Bobby said in what sounded like his official deputy voice. Then his face changed, and he pulled out his phone. He read whatever was on the screen and said something that they definitely don't teach you in preschool, and then he nudged me to let him out of the booth.

"What's up?" I asked as I slid out.

"I forgot," he said. "I'm late."

"Forgot what?"

"IS IT ANOTHER DATE?" Millie asked.

The music changed. It was Taylor Swift, which I felt was a stretch for Country Night, but I was too focused on Bobby's sudden departure to notice which song.

"I'll see you guys later," Bobby said. He gave the back of my head a quick scruff, almost pulling me into a hug, and then, with a wave for everyone else, he darted toward the door.

As I settled back into the booth, Fox said, "He's certainly in a hurry."

"Millie's right," I said. "Probably another hot date with another new guy. And we'll have to pretend to remember his name. And then, in another week, it'll be someone else."

Indira and Fox exchanged looks. Millie and Keme exchanged looks.

"What?" I asked.

Indira patted my hand again and said to Fox, "Could you give me a ride home?"

"Of course," Fox said. "Keme?"

The boy glanced at Millie, but she shook her head. "I've got to get home and pack up a couple of pieces I sold on Etsy."

Keme cocked his head.

"No, I don't need any help," Millie answered. "But thank you."

Keme looked like he was scrambling to come up with another, equally valid reason they should spend more time together.

With a little breath of a laugh, Fox caught his arm and said, "Come on."

The four of them left after settling up, and I paid my tab—and Bobby's, which was totally fair since if you counted all the donuts he brought me, I owed him a *lot* of money. I thought about ordering another drink—a gimlet, maybe. The thought surprised me, since it was one of those old-fashioned drinks that I associated with Chandler and Hammett and the like. At one point in my life, those had been my drinks of choice, but since moving to Hastings Rock, I'd found myself…branching out.

Only now, for some reason, a gimlet was on my mind. A noir drink for a noir night, I thought, which sounded too melodramatic even for me—but also, true. Because to my own surprise, my mood had soured. I couldn't put my finger on why, but it had. I thought about the look on Bobby's face when he read the message on his phone. The way he'd bumped his hip against mine to get me moving out of the booth. Those strong fingers running through my hair—the gesture playful, but also familiar. Maybe I did know why, I thought. Maybe that's why I wanted a gimlet.

Instead, though, I did the responsible thing: I got in the Jeep and started home. The night was chilly and damp, and although the sky was clear, I already knew the fog belt would be thick, and driving home meant heading straight into a world that became directionless, claustrophobic, a thousand shifting currents of gray that sparked to life in the headlights, with only the occasional silhouette of Sitka spruce and lodgepole pine to anchor the world. Normally, I loved the coast and the cool weather and the fog. It activated that innermost, geekiest part of me that loved haunted mansions and crumbling castles and, yes, werewolves and vampires. And maybe the moors? But maybe that was just because I had a crush on Heathcliff in *Wuthering Heights*.

I was so caught up in my thoughts that I didn't notice Bobby's Pilot until I was driving past it. The SUV was parked in the gravel lot of an apartment complex—in the dark, it was hard to tell the color of the shiplap siding, but it was blue or gray or blue-gray or something that might have been called "pewter tankard" on a paint swatch. The complex was only a few buildings, all of them unremarkable. I'd driven past them countless times on my way to and from

Hastings Rock, and I'd never given them a second look. Until now. When Bobby's car was parked there.

He's on a date, I thought. And my body's reaction was a flush that sent pins and needles to my chest, my neck, my face. I didn't even have to think about what *kind* of date it was. Or why Bobby had been in such a hurry. Or why he'd already be at the other guy's apartment. I mean, not that I was a prude. I'd hooked up with strangers before. Okay, I'd thought about hooking up with strangers before. Okay, I *would* have hooked up with strangers, except the one time I tried, I got so nervous that I had to pull over and puke on the side of the road, and I ended up messaging the guy (because of course I did, because I couldn't just ghost him) and telling him I couldn't, um, do adult stuff with him because I'd just watched *Jurassic Park III* and I was upset about how bad it had been.

But it was totally fine for Bobby to hook up with somebody. Anybody. Whoever he wanted. However many he wanted. Whenever he wanted. Even if the, um, booty call came when he was hanging out with friends. And trying to solve a murder. And I mean, it was totally fine for Bobby to do whatever he wanted, but was he even being safe? Not, like, that way. But if these were total strangers, shouldn't he be telling someone where he was going? What if they were axe murderers? What if they wanted to turn Bobby into a sock puppet? And if this guy *wasn't* a total stranger, then couldn't Bobby say something like, *Hey, tonight I'm hanging out with Dash and the gang because I haven't been spending enough time with them and they're my best friends?*

If you asked me, I'd say that's a sign of a toxic relationship, when your new boyfriend won't let you spend any time with your old friends.

Oh my God.

Did Bobby have a boyfriend?

Believe it or not, all of this went through my brain in about half a second. Which was perfect timing because a moment later, Bobby, another man, and a woman stepped out of one of the ground-floor apartments, and I almost drove off the road. I only caught a glimpse of them: the man looked young, blond, and ridiculously cute in a tee and jean shorts. The woman was older, with darker hair—maybe honey blond, I wanted to say, although it was hard to tell as she stepped away from the porch light. They were laughing about something, and as I watched, Bobby put his arm around the blond man's shoulders. The woman said something, and the blond beamed. The woman said something again, and this time, Bobby shook her hand. She said something that made them all laugh again as she pulled him into a hug.

And then I was past them, and then a moment later, I was past the apartment building, and I couldn't even see them in my rearview mirror. All I could see was myself, and the dark, and the empty road behind me, red with my taillights.

CHAPTER 6

The next morning, I stayed in the den (which, to judge by the number of crumpled-up sheets of paper, the abandoned pens, and the half-finished cups of coffee, was now starting to look more like a villain's lair than a writer's workspace). I stared at the screen of my laptop. The cursor blinked back at me.

Somehow, for some reason, I had let Hugo talk me into a co-writing project. When I put it like that, I make it sound like he was twisting my arm (which, kind of, he was). But the rational part of me also knew that it was a tremendous opportunity—Hugo was a published author, his star was rising, and he was doing me a favor (scratch that; he was handing me a winning lottery ticket) by letting me write with him.

And it didn't hurt that Hugo's arguments had been so persuasive. I mean, Hugo had been right: I'd been grappling with Will Gower, the imaginary detective who lived inside my head, for decades now. And so far, after about a million permutations, the idea hadn't gone anywhere. Why not try something new? Why not give Will Gower a break? I mean, authors did that all the time—they might start off with an idea that lived and grew with them for years and years, but at some point, practicality set in, and they moved on to an idea that they could, you know, actually sell. (Or, for that matter, actually write.)

And Hugo's idea was going to sell; I already knew that. *The Next Night* was an update on the noir genre, which was already well within my wheelhouse.

Private investigator Dexter Drake was caught in a loop created by systemic oppression, the realities of being a gay man in 1940s Los Angeles, and, of course, his own bad choices (a trademark of the hard-boiled and noir was the detective who was hampered by his inability to be anything but what he was).

It was...fun. I mean, it wasn't exactly my thing. But Hugo was basically a genius, and as he had told me—convincingly, many times—this was going to be a great way to stretch myself as a writer.

The only problem was that—speaking of the inability to be anything but what we are—writing Dexter Drake wasn't all that much easier than writing Will Gower.

Never mind, I texted Hugo, still staring at the blinking cursor on our shared doc. *I give up.*

His reply came a moment later—a GIF of a cat typing manically on a keyboard.

Nope, I wrote back. *I'm done. I'm finished. It's over. It never even began. Have you been talking to Fox?*

No. But that did remind me of some of Fox's more memorable fits of despair, so I riffed on some of those. *I'm a sham. I'm a huckster. My only success was a fluke, and everyone is going to see me for the fraud I am.*

This time, the composition bubbles appeared, disappeared, appeared, disappeared. And then, finally, Hugo's reply came through: *It's a description paragraph for a sleazy office. You don't have to write* War and Peace.

Which was a helpful reminder, sure. But I decided to stick with my guns. *This is what I'm talking about. I can't even come up with a simple description for a sleazy office.*

The next pause was even longer. But when Hugo replied, the composition bubbles appeared only briefly. There was no pausing. No erasing. Just a short, quick message. And then it came through: *Write what you see.*

I almost replied, *Easy for you to say.* But I held myself back. In the first place, because I knew—by this point—that I was feeling sorry for myself. But also because he was right. It was a description. That was all. And yes, it was easy for my brain to spin out of control even with something as simple as that—because in the best writing, a description was never just a description. A description was also a window into a character's mind, into how they perceived the world, their idiolect, their past, everything that shaped the process of perception and interpretation. What you saw in a simple passage of description, in the hands of a good writer, was the character, and the mood, and the theme, even the foreshadowed action—everything, in other words.

Write what you see.

The office was small and cramped and smelled like boiled cabbage. The desk was battered steel, painted the battleship gray Bobby remembered from the Army; every desk he'd ever seen, on every post and base where Uncle Sam had sent him, he'd seen that same desk. The papers covering the desk might be interesting, but what held his attention now was the blood—spattered across the desktop, and at one corner, thick and black in the weak light from the hall. Bobby stepped back, reached into the pocket of his windbreaker, and wrapped his hand around the little gun. Fear made his heart start to pound. On the wall opposite him, a cheesecake girl stared down at the scene from her poster, looking like all she wanted was to take a break and put her feet up.

With an explosion of breath like someone surfacing from a deep dive, I leaned back from the laptop. My brain was already circling around each sentence, jumping over words, scanning the text, probing for weaknesses. Were they called cheesecake girls? Pinup girls? A quick search told me that the term was cheesecake, not cheesecake girls, but I liked the sound of the phrase, so I decided to leave it—if someone wanted to buy the story and told me to change it, then I'd worry about it. I wasn't crazy about *boiled cabbage*. That was a good detail, but the blood smell seemed like it would be stronger, so I changed it to *rust*. And there was too much stage direction at the end; I took out the part about him *stepping back*. It was enough for him to put his hand in his pocket. Same with the heart-pounding fear (hello, cliché!). I deleted that whole sentence—if someone couldn't tell he was worried/concerned/afraid from the blood and the gun, I wasn't doing my job.

After those changes, it actually wasn't *terrible*. I mean, it did the job. But was *rust* really the right word? Maybe it should have been *rusting metal*? Or more vivid—maybe *smelled like his grandparents' garage, where they'd kept a rust-eaten Plymouth that had been full of moths*. Okay, I actually liked the image of the moths billowing out of the old Plymouth, so maybe just one more change—

But I stopped myself. This wasn't the right moment in the story—the focus needed to be here and now, not on the past. In the next chapter, maybe, when he was remembering the blood, he could associate it with the old Plymouth, with his first, startled discovery when a cloud of moths came pouring out of the old car.

Finally, I made myself text Hugo: *?*

His text came back a moment later: *There's my guy.*

I couldn't help but grin; there were a lot of things that hadn't worked in my relationship with Hugo, but he was a great writer, and there was something so…reassuring about having his approval. It was one of the reasons I'd agreed to write this story with him—Hugo knew how to handle me when I got tangled in my own thoughts, and he knew how to cut through the nonsense and get me back on track. (At least, most of the time.)

Then the next text came through: *When did we change his name to Bobby?*

Fortunately, texts don't automatically pick up your brain waves and translate them into words. Otherwise, Hugo would have gotten a message that looked something like this: *uhhhhhhhhhhhhhhhhhhhhhhhhhh*

It was easier to fix the problem than to examine it too closely. I went back and changed the name to Dexter; that's what we'd been calling our ex-Army gumshoe. Then I sent a text that said: *Sorry, I don't know what happened there.*

The silence on Hugo's end lasted almost a full minute before he replied, *Okay.*

Another message came through a moment later: *Ready to keep going?*

Oh. Right. The story.

I turned my attention to the screen, trying to remember what we'd discussed would happen next, but my brain kept flashing back to Bobby's name slipping out of my fingertips, and Bobby standing in the half-moon of the apartment building's porch light, and Hugo's silence until that single, horrible *Okay*.

I've spent a lot of my life wishing for catastrophes—you know, spontaneous sinkholes, an unexpected meteorite through the head (was it a meteor or a meteorite? I should definitely look that up), even something as banal as a heart attack. But, of course, those things never happened when you needed them. (Being abducted to be the bride of Sasquatch was my recent favorite, but believe it or not, the big hairy brute had never once crashed through the window and carried me off at an opportune moment. Not even the time Keme walked in when I was opening my new underwear. And I don't care what he tells you, they *do* make superhero-themed underwear for adult men.)

So, it was a tremendously gratifying surprise when something crashed upstairs.

I dashed—yikes!—off a text to Hugo that said, *Hold on, emergency*, and sprinted out of the den.

In the upstairs hall, I paused to listen. Sounds came from Bobby's room, and it took me a moment to recognize what I was hearing: something being dragged over a rug.

Since moving into Hemlock House, I'd had an unexpectedly high number of unwanted visitors—usually people who wanted to kill me. I guess that came with the territory of being an amateur sleuth, so I should have expected it, but let me tell you: it put a real damper on surprise parties. It also made me wary of investigating sounds I didn't recognize. I did a quick mental rundown: Keme would never have gone in Bobby's room without permission (in contrast to my room—see the story above), and neither would Millie or Fox or Indira. For that matter, as far as I knew, nobody else was home. Indira had gone to the farmer's market, and Bobby was working.

So, who was in his room?

Hugo.

No, I told my brain. That would make for a great twist if my life were a particularly soap-opera-y mystery novel, but it definitely wasn't Hugo.

Unfortunately, I didn't have any other flashes of inspiration.

I did, however, have a way to find out without barging in on a potential killer.

Here's a quick rundown on Hemlock House: it's big, it's beautiful, and it was built by a crazy man. All three of those statements are pretty much objective facts. Hemlock House was a sprawling manor that, by my best guess, had started off with a Georgian floor plan and then evolved through several phases until it had all the best Victorian eccentricities. It had damask wallpaper and parquet floors and chandeliers and fireplaces and so many oil paintings of horses. It had a LOT (in Millie-speak) of taxidermy animals, and if you looked closely, you could find a hedgehog smoking a pack of Lucky Strikes. It had bone china and silver mirrors and mantel clocks that every mystery writer dreams of turning into a murder weapon. And—to my eternal delight, because I'm a thirteen-year-old boy at heart and have never grown up—it was riddled with secret passages.

One of which I'd discovered when I'd been, uh, monitoring Keme.

(Monitoring sounds better than spying on, and, to be fair, Keme did need adult supervision, whether he believed it or not.)

A section of paneling in the servants' staircase opened easily when I pressed the catch hidden in one of the stiles. I slipped through the opening into a dusty hallway. For a moment, I worried about tipping my hand by leaving footprints; Keme didn't know I knew about this space, and I didn't want him to feel like I'd invaded his privacy. At the same time, he was a minor, and he slept here more often than he did at home—wherever home was, since Keme refused to tell me anything about that part of his life. And we (the rest of us) all agreed that, in spite of Keme's independence, he still needed, well, help. My fears about being caught didn't last long, though; Keme had tracked back and forth so many times that he'd cleared a path down the center of the secret passage, and my own steps wouldn't be visible.

I hurried down the narrow passageway—in some sections, the walls came so close together that I had to turn sideways to proceed. I passed an opening onto a small, octagonal room that was the top of one of the old house's turrets. Leadlights on each wall allowed a surprising amount of light into the space, making it feel open and airy despite its low ceiling, and I imagined it would be beautiful at night, too, looking out at the trees and the stars. The last time I'd snooped around back here, the turret room had been empty. Now, a sleeping bag was stretched out next to a bag of animal crackers, a physics textbook, and two different flashlights (one small, and one big). I stood there for a moment, my original mission forgotten. He'd been sleeping up here. Alone. With nothing but flashlights and a sleeping bag and the hard floor.

Okay, it was official. I was a terrible human being. Keme deserved better than this. The problem, though, was that Keme was fiercely independent—emphasis on the *fiercely*. I wanted to make things better for him. I just had no idea how to do it without alienating him completely.

But that was a problem to agonize over in the immediate future; right now, I had an intruder to catch.

I continued down the passage. After a few more yards, it turned; dusty windows gave glimpses of the back of the house: the twisted hemlocks, the waves breaking against the cliffs, and the stretched-out gray of the sea like a rumpled tarpaulin. The passageway seemed even darker after that glimpse of the outside world, and it only got darker as I moved farther away from the windows.

I passed a set of peepholes that, I knew from previous experimentation, allowed someone to look into my bedroom. (I'd addressed this problem by moving the tallboy to block them.) The next set of peepholes looked into the bathroom. (Yuck. It was the kind of thing that made it hard to feel sorry for

Nathaniel Blackwood; I was starting to suspect that the creep who had built Hemlock House had deserved to be pushed from the balcony by his child-bride.) And the next set looked in on Bobby's room.

In theory.

I mean, I wasn't enough of a creep to try them out and risk violating his privacy. And although I was now realizing that I probably should have told him about the peepholes as soon as I discovered them, at the time it had seemed like a nonexistent problem—I mean, if only Keme and I knew about this part of the house, then it wasn't an issue.

Now, as I slid open the peepholes, I was starting to suspect that however the next few minutes unfolded, Bobby was going to have...questions.

The peepholes were centered on one of the long walls of Bobby's bedroom, and they gave a surprisingly good view of the space. As usual, it was neat and clean to a degree that suggested military precision. (Not that Bobby had ever been in the military, by the way—he'd just picked up some of those undesirable habits like daily exercise, respect, and, uh, manliness?) What was *less* usual was the blond boy who was currently rifling Bobby's nightstand.

Boy, I realized on a second look, might not technically be accurate. After a longer look, I pegged him somewhere in his early twenties. He had creamy skin, a mop of blond hair, and thin eyebrows that were a darker blond than the hair on his head. A narrow jaw made his face interesting rather than classically handsome. He wore a cardigan with a tee and jeans, which wasn't exactly traditional cat burglar attire, but that didn't slow him down as he pulled the topmost drawer out of the nightstand and dumped it into a cardboard box. Then, without missing a beat, he grabbed the cardboard box and started toward the door at a jog.

I scrambled down the hall to the secret door that led into Bobby's room. On my side, it looked more or less like a standard door, with slightly unusual dimensions. But the other side, which faced the bedroom, was a mirror in a gilt frame. Which, I assume, made it even more dramatic when I flung the door open, jumped out of the secret passage, and picked up the closest thing at hand—based on a brief fling with historical fiction, I was fairly sure it was a coal scuttle—and shouted, "Stop! Thief!"

The young guy's head whipped around, and he ran straight into the door. The box he was carrying flew into the air, and he stumbled backward. Then he fell. Then he did this weird, backward half-somersault. And that's how he ended up on the floor, staring up at me, with a bloody nose. In a dazed voice, he mumbled, "You must be Dash."

"Uh, yes?"

(I know. It wasn't supposed to be a question.)

But the fact that he seemed to know me and didn't appear to be trying to run away (didn't even appear to be trying to sit up) made it hard to stay amped up. Just for good measure, though, I brandished the coal scuttle and asked, "Who are you?"

Pinching the bridge of his nose with one hand (apparently, he was an experienced nose-bleeder), he sounded slightly nasal as he extended one hand. "Kiefer Smith."

Uh oh.

In that instant, I realized why he (now, too late) looked slightly familiar—because this was the same guy I'd seen Bobby with outside the apartment building the night before.

"Oh my God," I said and bent down to help him.

And, in the process, I managed to almost clobber him with the coal scuttle.

"Oh my God," I said again, and after ditching the scuttle, I tried again. "I'm so sorry. Are you okay?"

He had a bewildered smile as he let me help him into a sitting position. "I ran into a door."

"I know. Oh my God." That was three times, and the writerly part of my brain suggested that was enough. "I'm so sorry, I didn't mean to scare you—well, I mean I did, but not because—I mean, I didn't know it was you—I mean,

I knew it was *you* because I saw you, but I didn't know who you were—" I could hear myself unspooling verbally. But when I stopped, the only thing I could come up with was "Oh my GOD!"

(Millie would have been proud.)

Kiefer only laughed, though. It was wet and, yes, a bit nasal because of the bloody nose, but it sounded surprisingly free of rancor. "It's okay. It's my dumb fault for not watching where I was going. Do you have a tissue? Bobby's going to kill me if I ruin this rug."

I caught myself about to explain that Bobby didn't care about rugs. Bobby didn't care about floor coverings of any kind, although he *was* really proud of the new bath mat he'd purchased. (He seemed to think that it was a real coup that he'd found one made of memory foam, which only further supported my theory that Bobby was a straight guy who had been switched at birth.) Instead, I hurried into the bathroom and got the whole box of tissues.

Kiefer accepted them with a smile and wadded them against his nose.

That was when I noticed the red mark on his forehead. At this point, I figured I might as well give into it, and I blurted, "Oh my God."

"Huh?"

"Your head!"

He touched his forehead, winced, and gave another smile. "Doesn't feel broken."

"Kiefer, I am *so* sorry." And then, before I could stop myself, I asked, "What were you doing?"

"Please don't tell Bobby."

I hadn't been expecting that. "Tell him what?"

"It was supposed to be a surprise." But the real surprise was when the tears started. "He's going to be so mad."

Which didn't make any sense because Bobby didn't *get* mad. I mean, sure, he wasn't thrilled when you told him you were going to do your writing for the day, only you had to use the bathroom, and then you needed a snack to keep your blood sugar up, and when he came back from his run, you were up to your ears in Indira's Black Forest cherry cake. And he definitely didn't like it if you got yourself accidentally, unfortunately, totally by chance caught up in a murder investigation, even if it wasn't your fault. Like, at all. But angry? That wasn't a word that came to mind when I thought of Bobby Mai.

Before I had to press for answers, words spilled out of Kiefer. "I just wanted to help him, you know. And I thought it would be cute to spend our first night there together, even if it was, you know, kind of rough."

He tentatively peeled the tissues away from his nose. They were crimson where they'd soaked up his blood, and his nose looked puffy. His eyes were still watery with some mixture of tears and pain, and I thought again that he looked like a boy. I looked at the box that he'd dropped and noticed, now, what had fallen free: Bobby's phone charger; his earbuds; his clock; a bottle of hand lotion. Everything, my brain registered, from his nightstand.

"Your first night together where?" I asked.

Kiefer wasn't looking at me. He dabbed at his nose with the tissues and gave an experimental sniffle. "Our new apartment."

I didn't remember sitting down, but my butt was on the floor, and I was staring at him, watching him study the bloody tissues as though they contained some kind of mystery. The crash of the waves was distant and rhythmic. Goose bumps broke out on my arms, and from a long way off, I remembered that Hemlock House could feel cold even at the height of summer.

A door shut in the distance, and then familiar footsteps rang out on the stairs. I sat where I was. It was like a horror movie. Or like a nightmare. All I could do was listen as the steps came closer: firm, confident, measured. Move, I thought. Or tried to think. But my head felt empty except for the crash and sigh of the waves.

The door opened, and Bobby stood there. He was dressed in his uniform. His black hair was in its usual perfect part. That first moment was one of the rare times I'd seen Bobby off balance, and I thought I glimpsed something in his expression that I didn't know how to read. And then his face closed again, and he crouched next to Kiefer.

"What happened?" he asked.

Kiefer launched into an explanation that didn't really explain anything. It mostly consisted of grabbing Bobby's arm and struggling with tears as he lurched back and forth through the sequence of events.

When he'd finished, Bobby looked at me.

"I thought someone had broken in," I said. And a nasty little voice inside my head said that someone *had* broken in—and that someone was right here. "I checked—" I gave a wave toward the still-open mirror door that I hoped would explain, nonverbally, the concept of *secret passage*. "—and I thought he was stealing your stuff."

Bobby's gaze moved to the fallen box and his personal items strewn across the floor.

"I thought it would be cute—" Kiefer began.

"He thought it would be cute," I said over him, "if you spent your first night together at your new apartment."

If you didn't know Bobby, you wouldn't have noticed his flinch.

"Please don't be mad," Kiefer babbled. "It was a stupid idea, and I thought it would be fun, and I never should have done anything without asking you. I know I shouldn't have touched your stuff—"

Bobby shushed him and spoke into the flow of words, stopping them with his usual calm. "I'm going to get you some ice for your nose." And then he paused, as though to give the next sentence its own weight, and said, "I'm not angry."

Kiefer was crying again, trying to catch the tears with the bloody tissues. Bobby let out a controlled breath and plucked clean ones from the box.

"I'll get it," I said. Somehow, my legs were still working, and I got to my feet. "I'll get the ice."

"No," Bobby said.

But too late.

He caught up with me on the stairs. "I'll take care of this," he said. "I'm sorry he interrupted your writing." He let out another of those controlled breaths. "And I'm sorry he frightened you. I know you've had bad experiences with people breaking into the house—"

"I wasn't frightened. I was concerned." At the bottom of the stairs, I made a sharp left. "And I took care of it."

"I'm sorry—"

"He seems sweet." And a vicious part of me wanted to say, *Just like West.* Somehow, though, I managed to say, "I'm sorry about all of this. Typical Dash, right? I botched the whole thing."

"You didn't botch anything. His nose isn't broken and—"

Another of those sharp little turns took me into the servants' dining room, and I shut the door behind me.

Bobby, of course, just kept coming. "—he's fine," he said as he came after me. "Would you slow down for a second? I'm trying to—"

But I was already passing into the kitchen, and I shut that door behind me too. Hard.

And Bobby barreled after me. At the refrigerator, he caught my arm. He didn't pull. He didn't even grip me particularly tightly. I stared at the refrigerator.

"I'm trying to talk to you," he said again. And then all that control began to unravel, and he said, "Really? You're not even going to look at me?"

I spun around, and in the process, I freed my arm and spoke in clipped, detached fragments. "I'm trying to get ice. For your boyfriend. Who's got a bloody nose. Because I startled him when he was packing up all your belongings so you could move into your new apartment!" The sentence had started off at a normal volume, but by the end it was a full-on shout. I kept shouting. "Were you going to tell me you were moving out? Or was I just going to get the last month's rent in the mail?"

"I don't pay you rent," Bobby said. "And of course I was going to tell you."

"Really? When?"

He opened his mouth.

"Last night, after you signed the lease?" I asked.

He shut his mouth.

"Or the week before that, when you were looking at apartments?"

He put his hands on his hips. It wasn't quite a slouch, since Bobby never slouched, but there was something insolent about the pose—a kind of juvenile *screw-off* so at odds with the Bobby I knew that I couldn't quite wrap my head around it.

"Or the week before that," I asked, "when you had your first date with Kiefer?"

Color rose under Bobby's smooth, golden-olive complexion. "I didn't meet him two weeks ago."

"Oh, right." I laughed. "Sorry. I must have gotten him confused with the guy before him. Or the one before that. It's hard to keep them all straight. Tell me, how long have you and Kiefer been dating?"

"You're being immature about this."

"I'm being immature? How long ago did you start dating him, Bobby? It's a simple question."

His jaw tightened. His slouch didn't look quite so relaxed anymore. The refrigerator hummed.

"Four and a half weeks—"

"A month," I said. "You've been dating him a month, and you're moving in with him."

"Yes."

I waited, but nothing more came. "That's it? That's all you're going to say?"

"We're in a relationship. It's serious. This is the next logical step."

"It's *serious*?" I couldn't keep control of my tone—or my volume. "Bobby, he's basically a teenager. How old is he? What's he doing with his life? How could you possibly know, after a month, that this relationship is serious?"

"He's twenty-two years old," Bobby said, and this time there was an edge in his voice I wasn't sure I'd heard before. "He's smart. He's passionate about—about a lot of things."

"Oh yeah? What's his middle name?"

Bobby cut his eyes away.

"Are you kidding me?" I asked.

More of that color rushed into Bobby's cheeks, but he still didn't look at me. "I guess you knew everything about Hugo before you moved in with him."

"No, I didn't know everything about him. But we'd been together for more than two years when we got our first apartment."

Now, his gaze slid back to me. "And that's fine, Dash. That worked for you. But every relationship is different. People move at different speeds in their relationships."

"What speed is this? Warp speed? Light speed?" I don't know why *Space Balls* was the first reference that came to mind, but it popped out of my mouth before I could stop it. "Ludicrous speed?"

"Not everyone is like you. Not everyone has to spend years evaluating every possible outcome before they'll even consider taking the first step in a relationship."

Something about the lights in the kitchen seemed off, like my pupils had dilated and couldn't quite correct. A second passed, and then another. "Wow."

"That's not what I meant."

"Yes, it is."

"No, Dash—" Frustration creased Bobby's brow. "I'm just saying that every relationship is a gamble. After a certain point, you're just making time, and you have to take a chance."

I nodded. My head felt loose on my neck. Stepping around Bobby, I started toward the servants' dining room.

He reached out like he might stop me, but his hand fell short. "Can we please sit down and talk about this? I'm really unhappy with how this conversation is going."

"What's there to talk about?" I asked. "You made your decision. Everything is—how did you put it? Everything else is just making time."

CHAPTER 7

For the first section of the drive, I was on autopilot. The brisk mid-morning of June on the Oregon Coast became a blur of still-damp ferns, pavement dark with moisture, the branches of spruce and pine and fir glistening. I passed Hastings Rock, with its jumble of architectural styles—everything from Victorian to beach bungalow to modernist—making a postcard skyline against the horizon. The Jeep, always noisy, seemed louder than usual, until the rush of wind against the frame and the roar of the engine made me feel like I'd stuck my head in a wind tunnel. In a good way, if that makes any sense.

But below that initial level of disconnect, I ran through frenzied replays of the conversation with Kiefer and Bobby. How Kiefer had said, *I thought it would be cute.* How Bobby had said, *Of course I was going to tell you.* The way he'd stood in the kitchen, that defiant pose like he knew he was doing something wrong and was daring me to say something about it. How he'd said, *Not everyone is like you.*

How dare you? That's what I wanted to say. And I wanted to—to shake him. It wasn't something I'd felt before, as though words weren't a sufficient outlet for my feelings. Like the only way I could tell him how I felt was to lay hands on him, as though somehow pure force could *make* him see that he was being an idiot. And even as I shook with the need, I was also horrified by the strength of that urge, by the darker current of it. Because I wanted to do something that would shock Bobby. I wanted to do something that would snap him out of this craziness. I wanted to do something that would wipe that stupid look off his face. You've known each other a month, I wanted to say. Barely a month. You don't even know his middle name. But what I really wanted to say, what was stuck in my throat, was: How dare you feel sorry for me?

Because that was what it had been at the end. Condescending, yes. Patronizing, sure. But worst of all, full of pity.

Not everyone is like you.

Fine, I thought. No problem. Move out. Go live a great, happy life with this baby version of West you somehow managed to dig up. See if it goes any better for you this time.

And then I started to cry. I had to pull onto the shoulder of the road, easing the Jeep to a halt. I didn't sob. I didn't fall apart. But I sat there, fighting wave after wave, my eyes hot and stinging.

Eventually, I got myself under control again. Slumped in my seat, I stared out the windshield. The day was bright and clear, and even inside the Jeep, I could tell it was warming up pleasantly—a perfect summer day in this part of the world. Next to me, green stalks rippled in the breeze. Barley, maybe. Or wheat. An ancient wheel line sprinkler broke up the neat rows. As I watched, a little brown bird with a yellow throat fluttered down onto the lateral pipe. It cocked its head, as though listening to something, and took off again in a flurry of movement.

The world moves on, I thought. And I checked the mirror and shifted into drive and got going again.

It would have been generous to call my sudden flight from Hemlock House a plan, but I *had* intended to talk to Neil and Jane Carver—or whatever Jane's last name was these days—and since I found myself almost halfway to Astoria, I decided now was as good a time as any.

When I got there, the street was as quiet and empty as it had been the day before. I drove past Arlen and Candy's house, but there was no sign of a grim-faced octogenarian lying in wait with a shotgun. Maybe more importantly, there was no sign of Candy, who probably would have asked me for Bobby's phone number. If she did, I was going to give it to her. Petty is as petty does.

Richard's house—which, I guess, was really Neil and Jane's house now—looked unchanged from the day before: a little white bungalow like all the others on the street. The curtains were open, and the windows were dark. I parked and got a look at the garage, but the door was down, and I couldn't tell if there was a car inside. Then I knocked on the front door.

Steps moved inside the house, and the door opened to reveal a woman. She was White, and I put her age somewhere in the sixties. She had long, thick hair that had once been dark but was graying now, and she had great skin—and clearly wasn't wearing any makeup. Not beautiful, but…well, what I might have called arresting, if I were writing about her. Something about her face held the eye. She wore a knit top, polyester slacks, and sensible pumps; she didn't seem like the type to lounge about the house in a muumuu.

Her voice was surprisingly deep when she said, "May I help you?"

"My name is Dash Dane. I'm sorry to bother you, but I'm looking for Jane Carver."

"I'm Jane Carver."

Believe it or not, there isn't a WikiHow article for "How to Introduce Yourself to a Potential Murderer." (I checked.) So, I said, "I know this is going to sound strange, but I was wondering if I could talk to you about Richard Lundgren. I'm not a reporter. This is going to sound crazy, but—"

"I know who you are, Mr. Dane. Won't you come in?"

"Uh, yes?"

(Will Gower definitely wouldn't have let it sound like a question.)

The living room at the front of the house was surprisingly updated and, if I'm being honest, beautiful. I mean, the size and the layout made it hard to pretend the house itself was anything but what it was, but Jane had done a great job with what she was working with. The sofa set was cream-colored upholstery with nailhead trim, and when Jane indicated for me to sit, I discovered that it was comfortable as well as attractive. The coffee table was simple—just solid wood with a good stain—but it matched the entertainment center. A few stylishly antiquated prints hung on the walls, and it took me a moment to recognize the watercolors as cityscapes of Astoria. Peonies exploded out of a blue glass vase and lent a hint of their perfume. It was a far cry from Arlen and Candy's place next door.

Jane left. Sounds filtered to me from the kitchen: running water, the clink of cups, steps moving back and forth. It took me a moment, but then I spotted the opportunity she'd given me, and I eased myself up from the sofa. The house was tiny, and a little stub of a hall connected the living room to the kitchen. I figured if Jane asked why I was wandering around, I could explain I was looking for the bathroom. That *never* went wrong in books.

Three doors stood open along the hallway. One connected with what had to be Jane and Neil's room—it had a lived-in look. The furniture here was dated but in good condition, and although the tops of the dresser and the wardrobe appeared to be free of the usual junk that tended to accumulate (at least, in my bedroom), one of the nightstands held books, and the other had an empty glass and a remote control. The next room was the small but pristine bathroom, with the same white tile running across the floor and up the walls. The shower curtain was closed, but if I pushed it back, I expected I'd find the tub scoured within an inch of its life. And the next room appeared to be for guests. The bed was made up, but it felt unused in a way that the other room hadn't. In the kitchen, a kettle whistled, and I started to turn back toward the living room. And then I noticed the books.

The bookcase stood against the far wall, and the books lining it were clearly all from the same series. I didn't need to get closer to know what they were; I'd read those books plenty of times, and I had the same series back at Hemlock House. They were the Matron of Murder books—Vivienne's *magnum opus*.

As the sound of footsteps moved closer, I hurried back to the living room and settled onto the sofa again. A moment later, Jane appeared, carrying a rosewood tray with a tea service for two. I watched her movements as she poured: steady, unhurried, assured.

"Milk? Sugar? Lemon? It's a Darjeeling that I just found."

"No, thanks."

She offered me a flash of a smile as she sat. "Excellent. I'd hate for you to ruin a good cuppa."

"It'd be a different story if it were coffee, though."

"Is that so?"

"Have you ever heard of a s'mores latte?"

With a quiet laugh, she shook her head. "I don't think my doctor would approve." She sipped her tea, watching me over the rim of the cup. And then she said, "You're trying to learn what happened to Richard."

"Yes."

She was silent for what felt like a long time—no longer sipping her tea, but holding the cup in both hands as though trying to absorb its warmth. "It happened a long time ago," she finally said. "It was a tragedy; Richard was a wonderful man. But tell me, Mr. Dane, why it matters now, after all these years? What good will come from opening old wounds?"

It was a strange metaphor, on top of a strange response. I wasn't sure what I'd been expecting—outright hostility, perhaps, like Arlen. I probably wouldn't have been too surprised by a distraught widow, complete with waterworks. But I hadn't expected this composed, reserved, and clearly intelligent woman whose first response was to ask why I was bothering to try to find her husband's killer. And I certainly hadn't expected the question to be…genuine, because it was clear that Jane wanted an answer.

"There are a few reasons, I guess," I said, trying to frame my response. "One is that Richard's killer is still walking around out there. He might have hurt other people. He might still be hurting other people. And even if he hasn't, he needs to be held accountable for what he did to Richard. I think that's what the family of every victim wants."

"Do you think so?" She seemed to contemplate her own question. "I don't know. Revenge is a hollow thing, and punishment isn't much better. We want what everyone wants, of course, which is for the awful thing never to have happened in the first place. But that's impossible." Her gaze focused on me again, as though she'd remembered me, and more crisply, she added, "Besides, this person might be dead. Might have died years ago. Or perhaps this person has lived an exemplary life. Perhaps they've gone on to do wonderful things, helped lots of people, and made the world a better place. Shouldn't all of that be weighed in the balance?"

"That's for a judge to decide. But Daniel Webster said justice is the ligament that holds a civilization together—I'm paraphrasing—and I think there's something to that. As a society, we agree to protect each other, and when we fail in that, we have a responsibility to make sure that order is restored."

"Injustice anywhere is a threat to justice everywhere."

"Something like that."

"But is it your responsibility, Mr. Dane?"

"Maybe not. But I don't know if there's anybody else. From what I understand, the police already think they know who did it. They're convinced Richard was one of Vivienne's first victims, but it doesn't seem so clear cut to me." I waited, but she didn't take the bait. She sat there, watching me, her dark eyes unreadable. "Don't you want justice for Richard? Aren't you angry?"

She set the teacup down, and it rattled against the saucer. Then she clasped her hands in her lap. "I've spent the last thirty years being angry with Richard. That doesn't make sense, I know. Perhaps you're right. Perhaps I should feel some sort of demand for justice. But I don't. I feel tired, Mr. Dane. And old. And empty. I don't know if I have it in me to feel that much anger again."

Silence fell over the little house. Outside, in the distance, a lawnmower came to life.

"Ask your questions, Mr. Dane," she said, and she took a tissue from her pocket and wiped her eyes. "I'd like to get this over with if you don't mind."

"Could we start with the night Richard disappeared?"

"We had a terrible fight. I left. When I came home, he was gone."

"What did you fight about?"

She gave a bitter laugh. "We fought about what we always fought about: Richard's stubbornness."

I waited, but she didn't expand on that. "I hate to ask this, but were you having an affair?"

"You've been talking to Candy." But she sounded amused more than anything. "No, Mr. Dane. I wasn't having an affair. And I imagine I know what your next question will be. I went to Neil's house after the fight; by that point, he and Vivienne had divorced, but he was still my friend, and I didn't have anywhere else to go. We weren't sleeping together, just to be clear."

"But you're married to Neil now."

"I understand the implication, Mr. Dane. Let me show you something." She excused herself and returned a moment later with a framed photo.

The colors were oversaturated and faded, and to judge by the clothes, it was from sometime in the 1970s or 80s. There were four people in it: two men and two women. It was easy to make out a young Vivienne and Richard—when I saw them together in the photo, the likeness was even stronger, although the Richard in this photo was even younger than the one in the photo Vivienne's attorney had sent me. The other two were clearly Neil, with his dark hair and dark eyes, and Jane. I guessed that the picture had been taken in a high school gym, because they sat on bleachers, Richard and Neil in basketball jerseys and skimpy shorts, their faces flushed and sweaty. Vivienne sat next to Neil in a sweater and slacks; she was one pearl necklace away from looking like a teenage June Cleaver. But Jane was perhaps the most surprising, radiant in makeup and a cheerleader uniform.

"We were friends," Jane said, turning the photo so she could look at it. "Best friends. Of course, everything seems more powerful at that age, but we really were close. It's hard to describe; have you ever had something like that? A group of people that you knew you belonged to, in a way that went beyond blood and bone?" A smile turned the corner of her mouth. "I believe young people today call it 'found family.'"

I nodded, and I was surprised to find myself explaining, "Here. In Hastings Rock, I mean. We call ourselves the Last Picks, like—"

"The last picks in gym," Jane said, and she laughed. It was a rich sound, deep like her voice, and full of unexpected delight. "Oh God, Vivienne must have loved that. She hated gym."

I grinned, but it was as much because of how surreal this moment felt as because of the statement itself. Here I was, with a woman double my age, listening to her talk about *the* Vivienne Carver as though she were just another hapless teenager. Which, I suppose, at one point she'd been, but it still felt unreal.

"After Neil and Vivienne divorced, we all wanted to stay friends. Neil's estranged from his family; he barely made it through high school without getting kicked out of the house, and once he left, he never went back. And he and Arlen hit it off right away. He was the son Arlen always wanted. After the divorce, Neil stayed part of the family." She stopped and cleared her throat. "I understand it must seem strange that Neil and I ended up together, but it really wasn't. Richard was gone. Vivienne had moved away. We had always been close." That unexpected smile turned the corner of her mouth again. There was something...self-aware about the smile. Not quite mocking, but close. "And, of course, I'd had a crush on Neil myself at one point in high school, although at the time, I couldn't see that he wasn't interested in me."

There were so many things I wanted to ask. I picked the first one that came to mind. "What did you mean that Neil was the son Arlen always wanted?"

Jane frowned. Her hands curled protectively around the picture frame, and she seemed to think. "Richard and Arlen's relationship was...difficult. They fought a great deal. Richard was temperamental. Arlen was stubborn. By the time I knew them, they'd settled into a pattern that was, let's say, antagonistic. Arlen commanded. Richard defied. Neil, on the other hand, has always been a charmer. As I said, he and Arlen hit it off right away."

"But you and Richard bought a house next to Arlen and—what was the mom's name?"

"Betty. She was already dying when Richard and I got married. Lung cancer. Richard wouldn't talk about living anywhere else, and then, once she was gone, we were settled. Richard had a job at the plant with Arlen, and I was at the teacher's college. It didn't make sense to move."

"They were close, then?"

"Oh yes. Richard was the apple of Betty's eye. He could do no wrong. Of course, that only made things worse with Arlen."

"Because he was temperamental."

"Yes." I thought maybe she'd stop there, but she sighed and looked past me, or through me, her eyes softening as they lost focus. "Richard was such a beautiful person. Everyone was drawn to him; it's hard to explain, hard to help someone understand. He was magnetic, to borrow a tired word. He was smart and funny. He made you feel like you were the only person who existed. And he was handsome too; he could have cut a swath through the ladies if he'd wanted to, but that wasn't his style."

"Maybe I was projecting," I said, "but I got the impression that the four of you were your own little group."

Jane laughed. "That we were unpopular, you mean? No, not at all. Vivienne might have been, if not for the rest of us. No. But we were...self-contained. Even back then, it irked some of our classmates. People tend not to like people who work their way free of the herd, so to speak. But it was impossible not to like Richard."

"But you fought frequently."

"Candy's information again?" she said. "Yes. In the last year or two before Richard went missing, we fought often. I hate to think about it now." Her voice caught, and she touched the tissue to her eye again. "I hate thinking about all of it. How unhappy we both were. How we took it out on each other."

"If you weren't fighting about an affair, what were you fighting about?"

"I'm afraid I was being glib when I said Richard's stubbornness. We fought about the usual things, of course. There was never enough money; even back then, the plant was cutting hours, and I still hadn't started teaching. And Richard—" She stopped. "How well did you know Vivienne? Before, I mean."

"Not well."

Jane nodded slowly. "She and Richard might as well have been twins. They were what we call Irish twins, as a matter of fact, although I suppose that's not the polite thing to say anymore. When Vivienne wanted to, she could be just as charming as Richard—she had that same magnetism, for lack of a better word."

I nodded; I remembered my first day at Hemlock House, and how easily Vivienne had won me over. It had been her hallmark during her years in the public eye—she was always kind, always polite, always witty, always easy to talk to.

"But Vivienne and Richard were never satisfied. They always wanted more. It was hard to see it at the time. When you're young, you think opportunities are endless, and that the world will give you what you deserve if you work hard enough. As they got older, though, and those opportunities didn't come to fruition, they changed. They were more jaded about things. They were more insistent. It was like a constant demand for more." She stopped again, and her eyes seemed to refocus on me. "That was one of the reasons for the divorce. Vivienne wanted Neil to uproot their lives and move to Portland. She was determined to be famous, whatever it took."

There was a lot packed into those words. In Vivienne's case, *whatever it took* had included framing an innocent woman for murder and, later in her life, killing two men to protect her secret.

"What did Richard want?" I asked.

"The same thing," Jane said with that same smile bent out of true. "Only different. Everyone who wants to be famous really just wants to be someone else."

The sound of the lawnmower cut off, and in its absence, the quiet pressed in on me. I tried to come up with a good way of asking my question, and finally I settled for simple: "What do you think happened the night Richard disappeared?"

But Jane shook her head. "You mean, do I think Vivienne killed him and stole our money and ran off to Portland?"

"I understand Vivienne and Richard were fighting as well."

"Richard was fighting with everyone. He was…not himself that last year. He was deeply unhappy." Jane blew out a breath. "I'm not sure what Candy told you, but I think I should say that, like the rest of that family, she's a deeply unhappy person. Some of that has to do with the fact that Candy has had a hard life, and it hasn't made things easier for her to watch Vivienne's success. That must have been very difficult for her. But it doesn't excuse this kind of behavior."

"What kind of behavior?"

"Making up stories. This whole mess she's created."

"What did she make up? I mean, I understand that not all her conclusions were correct, but it seems like what she told me was more or less true."

"You don't understand. You're not part of this family, so you don't understand. Nobody believes Vivienne killed Richard. I told you: they were like twins. She never would have hurt him, no matter how much they argued. Vivienne loved him more than she ever loved anyone else—"

The door handle rattled, and then the door swung open, and a man stepped into the living room. Today, Neil Carver wore a blue T-shirt with the words

ASTORIA FIRE DEPARTMENT on the breast and black utility pants. His hair looked thinner up close, and in that first instant, he carried himself the way Bobby sometimes did at the end of a long shift—like the fatigue went deeper than the bone. Then he saw me.

"What's he doing here?"

Which was interesting, albeit rude—apparently, everyone in the extended family knew who I was.

"He wanted to talk," Jane said quietly.

Neil spared her a disbelieving look. Then, to me, he said, "I don't know what you think you're doing, but you need to leave."

"I understand this is a difficult time for all of you," I said, "and I also understand this might be hard to believe, but I'm trying to help—"

"You're snooping around," Neil said, "playing detective. That's a job for the police."

Okay, again, fair, but definitely rude.

I looked at Jane, but her expression was closed off, and I realized she wasn't going to help. "I was hoping you could tell me about Richard, maybe about the night he disappeared—"

"He didn't disappear," Neil said. "He was killed. Aren't you ashamed of yourself? Don't you have the tiniest bit of decency? He was her husband. Their brother and son." He swallowed, and his voice wavered. "My best friend."

"I know, but—"

"If you know, then what are you doing? You're like a hog, rooting around in our suffering for your own entertainment. What kind of person does that?"

"Vivienne asked me to help—"

"Vivienne." He scoffed. "Vivienne doesn't need anyone's help. She made that perfectly clear when she left."

"Mr. Carver, do you honestly think she killed Richard?"

"Don't be ridiculous."

"The police do. And maybe it doesn't bother you to have Vivienne convicted of a crime she didn't commit—"

"Does it bother *you*?" He peered at me, and I realized, after a moment, he wanted an answer, but he continued, "What are you doing helping her anyway?"

"Yes, it does bother me. Because if she didn't kill Richard, then someone else did, and that person is still out there." I took a breath. "Candy seems to believe—"

"Candy." Neil pushed a hand through his thinning hair. "Candy is nuts."

In a soft voice, Jane said, "Neil."

"She is. He ought to hear that before he makes a fool of himself on her behalf." Squaring up with me, Neil continued in a more even tone, "All Candy wants is approval, just like Viv, just like Richard. Just like their old man—that's where they get it from. Can you understand that? Candy's spent her whole life making a fool out of herself to get people to notice her, running after any guy who would give her the time of day, and half the ones who wouldn't, myself included. She hates Viv because Viv went and made herself famous. She hated Richard because everyone loved Richard, never mind all the times Richard pulled her bacon out of the fire."

"Neil," Jane said again more firmly.

"He did. Not that she ever thanked him for it. You ought to hear her carrying on sometimes, how Richard ruined her life, chasing off that deadbeat. Everything that ever went wrong for Candy happened because Richard wouldn't let her shack up with Zane Potthof. He'd have had her turning tricks by the end of the week."

Jane straightened in her chair. "That's enough."

"She was thrilled when Richard disappeared. Ask *her* where she was the night Richard died."

"Neil!"

Jane's voice rang out in the small house. A hint of color dusted Neil's cheekbones, and he rubbed his forehead.

"I think it's time for you to leave," Jane said to me.

Neil gave ground grudgingly as Jane walked me to the door. He stood behind her, watching me as I moved out onto the porch, his expression somewhere between wary and chagrined. Jane's expression, though, was downright icy; the intelligent, pleasant woman I'd been talking to before Neil arrived was gone.

"Mr. Dane," Jane said as she shut the door. "Don't come back."

CHAPTER 8

I sat in the Jeep and watched the two houses.

Nobody came out and told me to leave. Nobody chased me off with a shotgun. With the window down and the sun on me, it was warm enough for me to shed my hoodie. The occasional breeze brought the smells of fresh-cut grass and gasoline and the darker undernote of the slough. Sunlight glittered on the windows of the houses I was watching. In Arlen's house, the curtains were closed.

The conversation certainly hadn't gone as I'd planned. In the first place, I'd been surprised by Jane—I'd been expecting another Candy, but instead, I'd found someone much more like the Vivienne I knew: composed, classy, and scarily smart. I'd also been surprised by what Jane had shared about the close-knit group of friends. It was hard to imagine Vivienne as an awkward teenager—although she hadn't looked particularly awkward in the photo Jane had shown me—but it wasn't hard to imagine that in a working-class town like Astoria, a bright, bookish girl might have struggled to find her place. And, once she'd found it, clung tightly to it. Jane was certainly a kindred spirit, and in spite of Neil's bad temper, it wasn't hard to imagine him and Richard as the kind of boys who were athletic and popular while still being, well, likable and intelligent human beings. All of it was a far cry from the picture Candy had painted of divorce, infidelity, rage, and greed, culminating in a sordid murder for a few thousand dollars.

But, at the same time, Jane's initial response to my appearance had been strange. Her questions about justice, about why I was bothering, weren't the questions I expected from someone who had been grieving her missing husband for decades. And Neil had been downright hostile when he arrived. It was hard not to wonder about the man who had stepped into Richard's life: Richard's home, Richard's wife, even wearing Richard's bracelet—or one that looked a lot like it. It might not be a glamorous life, but people killed for all sorts of reasons, and it was hard for me not to consider Neil, especially in light of his reaction, as a very real suspect.

What had I learned? Well, not much. Everything Jane had told me about the group of friends growing up had been good background information, sure, but I couldn't tell how much bearing it might have on the actual investigation. Jane had confirmed part of Candy's version of events—the change in Richard's behavior, the frequent arguments, and of course, the fight that had happened the night Richard disappeared. She'd provided an alibi for the night in question—Neil—that I was sure Neil would be happy to confirm. But perhaps most interesting of all was her insistence (and Neil's) that Vivienne hadn't killed Richard.

So, that was one point of interest: Jane (and Neil) painted a very different picture of Vivienne than Candy did.

And the second had been Neil's explosive comments about Candy. About her hatred of Richard. Blaming him for ruining her life. And that parting shot—*Ask* her *where she was the night Richard died*. I would have liked to ask a few more questions about Candy, but that seemed not to be an option; Jane's reaction to Neil's comments was as interesting as Neil's comments themselves. Why had Jane gotten so worked up about Candy? Or about what Neil was saying about Candy? Whatever it was, it had affected the polite, receptive woman so strongly that she'd told me never to come back.

Well, there was someone I could ask.

I got out of the Jeep and jogged across the street again, but this time, I approached Arlen's house. I knocked. No answer. I knocked again. Nothing. From the next block came the sound of a car engine and a rattling muffler.

If no one was home, I could—theoretically—take a look at the garage and the workshop. It would be remarkable if I suddenly discovered evidence that not only had the police overlooked but nobody had bothered to clean up in the last thirty-odd years, but I also couldn't shake the memory of Arlen popping out with his shotgun when Bobby and I had inspected the slough. Of course, searching the garage also sounded like a great way to get my head blown off. I'd be trespassing. I'd be committing a crime. Even if Arlen didn't shoot me himself, he could call the police. Indira would love to get a phone call asking to bail me out. No, searching the garage in the middle of the day, when I wasn't sure if anyone was home, seemed like a terrible idea. If Bobby had been there, he would have told me so. At length. And if I did it anyway, he would have been furious.

That made something poke its head up at the back of my brain.

On the other hand, I thought carefully, I was *pretty* sure Arlen's house was empty, and the street was dead. I hadn't seen a car or a pedestrian on either visit. So, this might be my golden opportunity. And if I missed it, I might never have another chance.

There it was: decision made. It was a carefully thought out, rational, pragmatic decision.

It had absolutely nothing to do with the fact that it would make Bobby insane when I told him.

I took the stairs down from the stoop two at a time and hustled around the side of the house. The gravel drive crunched underfoot, and from farther off came the slow stirring of the slough—just the occasional ripple-eddy-splash. The garage had the same sagging aluminum siding as the bungalow (with even more algae), and it looked like the roof hadn't been replaced since Sputnik. The overhead door was down, and a quick walk around the structure told me there wasn't a regular door—what I'd recently learned, while writing with Hugo, was called the pedestrian door. I gave up on the garage for the time being and continued to the workshop. This one *did* have a pedestrian door (I mean, a regular door), but it was locked. Someone had drilled one hole through the door and another through the plank wall and then run a chain through, and the chain was held shut with a padlock.

Well, well, well. Someone *really* didn't want people exploring the workshop.

I did another quick pass, but I didn't see any easy way into the single-story building. I considered the tire iron from the Jeep—the plank walls looked like they were of the variety that the Big Bad Wolf was in the habit of knocking down—but I gave it up. I'd probably be able to get inside the workshop, but I'd never be able to disguise the fact that someone had broken in. Besides, now that the thrill of making Bobby lose his mind had worn off, I was starting to suspect that I was behaving, er, injudiciously.

Halfway back to the Jeep, I caught a flicker of movement out of the corner of my eye. When I glanced over, I realized it had come from Arlen's house. From one of the windows, to be precise. I stared, but now the hideous curtains hung perfectly still. I was sure I hadn't imagined it—I'd seen those curtains move, if only briefly. And that meant someone was inside that house. I considered knocking once more, but I gave that up too; if they'd wanted to talk to me, they would have answered the first time.

When I started the Jeep and caught a look at the time, I was shocked by how late it was. The day had already been well underway before I'd heard Kiefer rummaging around upstairs, and between the argume—uh, conversation with Bobby, and then the drive to Astoria, the interview with Jane and Neil, and now my extracurricular activities, it was after six. The sun was sinking toward the horizon. In another hour, it would be cool again, and once the sun set, it might even verge on chilly.

A tiny part of me—miniscule, really, so small it didn't even deserve to be noticed—wondered if Bobby would be worried because I'd been gone so long.

I started back to Hastings Rock, alone with my thoughts. I passed the agricultural fields, where the neat rows of crops were bathed in golden light, and their long shadows looked like stencil work on the ground. A bird—a big one, a bird of prey—circled in the sky like a question mark being written, its wings barely seeming to move as it floated above me. Slowly, farmland shrank and gave way to the rocky coast. Spruce and fir and pine bristled along the edges of the road. It was such a nice day, I lowered the windows, and the smell of cedar and balsam came in on the evening's crisp breeze. The ocean shone like brass, and the lines of the waves looked like the hot tip of a soldering iron.

When my phone buzzed, it was almost like I'd been expecting it. Bobby's name showed on the Jeep's media console. I considered rolling up the windows—it would have been the polite thing to do—but I didn't.

I answered with a classic: a nice, friendly "What?"

Bobby's silence lasted a beat. "Where are you?"

"In the Jeep."

It felt like his pause was longer this time (which was very satisfying). "I'm having a hard time hearing you. Could you roll the windows up?"

"What do you want, Bobby?"

"I want to know where you are."

"I'm in the Jeep. Didn't we already have this conversation?"

The silence was definitely more significant this time. Then he said, "I understand you're upset—"

"Great. We've covered all our bases, then. I'm in the Jeep. I'm upset. And you, as usual, know everything."

"Did you drive up to Astoria by yourself?"

"I don't know, Bobby. Maybe."

"You don't know?"

"I don't know!" That was a little less cool, calm, and collected than I liked, so I took a deep breath. "You know what? I don't have to tell you where I am. I don't have to check in and report my location and keep you up to date on everywhere I go. Just like—"

I thought I could hear his frustrated exhalation, even with the wind whipping through the Jeep.

"—you don't have to tell me when you're moving out," I finished. "That's not the kind of friendship we have, it turns out. And that's okay. As long as we both understand the parameters of our friendship."

"I'm sorry you found out that way," Bobby said. But then he ruined it by adding, "Kiefer's sorry too. I'd like to talk to you—"

"Kiefer's sorry too." A laugh ripped its way out of me. "Okay, Bobby. Goodbye."

"Are you coming to sandcastle practice?"

Somehow, that hurt more than the rest of it. He wasn't worried, a little voice said inside my head. He wasn't fretting. Concern wasn't eating him up as he moped around the house. Instead, he'd been going about his day like normal. With Kiefer. It probably wasn't until I hadn't shown up for stupid sandcastle practice that he'd even wondered where I was.

"You know what—" I began.

Then sunlight flared in the rearview mirror: a flash of gold that left a spot dancing in my vision. Then the light was gone. It took me a moment to realize that the light had bounced off a truck that had come up behind me while I'd been on the phone. And now it was trying to pass me.

Returning my attention to the call, I tried to summon up whatever nasty thing I'd been about to say. But movement in my peripheral vision drew my attention again. The truck was speeding up as it tried to pass me. My automatic reflex was to ease my foot off the gas. In the low evening light, the driver was nothing more than a shadow. I made an impatient gesture for them to hurry up, and the truck's engine roared in response.

And then the truck swerved across the center line. I had an instant of clarity, when I knew it was going to hit me. Then the truck connected with the side of the Jeep. Metal shrieked. Rubber squealed. A fountain of sparks sprayed up. Instinct took over, the primitive need to get away. I yanked the wheel to the right, and too late, I realized my mistake. The shoulder dropped off abruptly, and a moment later, the Jeep rolled over and began its tumble toward the ocean.

Chapter 9

Strapped into my seat, all I could do was clutch the steering wheel as the Jeep rolled over again, and again, and crashed its way down the steep slope. The airbags exploded almost instantly, followed by the smell of burning fabric. I clipped a baby lodgepole pine, and the impact shook the Jeep and whipped my head to the side. It slowed us for a moment, and then with a vast, splintering sound, the lodgepole snapped, and the Jeep kept going. My field of view spun: trees, sky, water, trees, sky, water—

And then the Jeep hit a rock hard enough to shake my teeth in their sockets. I wasn't sure how much time passed before I processed the fact that we were no longer moving. Adrenaline buzzed through me, making me feel like I was floating, but I forced myself to take stock of the situation. That floating feeling, it turned out, was because the Jeep lay on its side, and I was dangling from my seat by the seatbelt. I'd lost my glasses, but even so, I still had a pretty good view of the ocean on the other side of the windshield—it was almost at eye level, which gave me an idea of how close I'd come to my, uh, final destination. Twisting around—and fighting gravity in the process—I managed to get a look out my side window. Pine needles blocked my line of sight, poking in where I'd had the window down, and it took me a moment to understand that the lodgepole pine I'd taken out in my slide to the bottom had somehow ended up on top of the Jeep.

Which was pretty much perfect.

Until, of course, the sound system crackled, and Jimmy Buffett came on, singing about Margaritaville.

It lost the Bluetooth signal, the rational part of me thought. That's why it switched over to the radio.

That was when the adrenaline ran out. I started to shake. The aches of bruised flesh and wrenched joints crowded forward. The seatbelt bit into me where it supported my weight. I fumbled with the buckle, braced one foot against the passenger seat, and got myself free. I was shaking harder now, so I eased myself down until my feet rested on the passenger window and I could sit on the center console. A moment later, my stomach lurched, and I had to fight down the need to do some *Exorcist*-style ralphing.

When the worst of the nausea faded, I wiped the cold sweat from my face and tried to pull myself together. I found my glasses in the footwell, miraculously unbroken, and put them on. Without the rush of adrenaline, my body hurt worse than ever, and I had the fragmented thought that I might be in shock. Get out. That seemed like a clear thought too. You need to get out of here.

The passenger door wasn't an option, since it was pressed flat against the ground, so I climbed up toward the driver door. The airbags had already deflated, so I pushed them out of my way. When I got to the door, it opened, which meant it hadn't gotten warped during the crash, but after about a quarter inch, it hit the tree that had fallen on top of us. The lodgepole couldn't have been that big—since *it* had snapped rather then, well, snapping *me*—but it was still too heavy for me to lift. I rolled the window down further (amazingly, that worked too) but all I got for my efforts were more pine needles in the face. Even pushing the smaller branches out of the way, I couldn't clear an opening big enough for me to crawl through. A quick glance toward the back of the Jeep didn't offer any help either. The tailgate didn't have an interior latch, and the window had shattered and showed only a blank face of rock now. I turned back to the front of the Jeep and gave the windshield a few kicks—it worked in books and movies sometimes—but didn't have any luck. If it *was* possible to kick out a windshield, I certainly wasn't going to be able to do it. I decided to blame it on the lack of leverage.

I was trapped.

A few minutes of searching told me that my phone was lost. (Jimmy Buffett had been replaced by Tom Petty's "Free Fallin'," and I didn't appreciate the universe's sense of humor.) So, I couldn't call for help. I had enough presence of mind now to turn off the engine, and the music cut out. I checked myself in the visor mirror, which felt weirdly vain, but aside from a red patch of skin, which I guessed was the airbag equivalent of rug burn, I was okay. I'd even escaped without the airbag breaking my nose, which seemed like a staple of the car accident genre. My body, on the other hand, was a different story. I felt like a doll that had been pulled apart and put back together again by an overenthusiastic toddler—everything done with unnecessary force, and nothing going back in the way it should have. My neck and head worried me the most; what had started as a low-grade headache in the accident's immediate aftermath was turning into something much uglier, and if I had the choice, I didn't want to be here when it arrived.

I wasn't a Boy Scout, but having dated Hugo for years had its advantages—I found the first aid kit, which had miraculously stayed under the seat where I'd stored it. I found some Tylenol, dry-swallowed it, and made myself as comfortable as I could to wait. The problem was that it might be a while; the Oregon Coast wasn't densely populated, and while it was our busy season, true, with tourists jammed into every available motel and Airbnb, this wasn't exactly a highly trafficked stretch of road. Sooner or later, though, someone would see the torn-up shoulder, the damaged trees, and the overturned Jeep, and they'd call emergency services.

But would they see me in the dark?

I didn't want to risk starting the Jeep—I had no idea what kind of damage it had taken, and for all I knew, I was sitting in the middle of a lake of gasoline.

I hit the hazard lights. Maybe later, once full dark had fallen, I could run the headlights off the battery. For a while, anyway.

Caught up in these thoughts, I was surprised by another realization: whoever had hit me had done so on purpose. There wasn't any other explanation. That truck hadn't veered into me by accident; it had rammed me, forcing me toward the shoulder and the precipitous drop. It took a little longer for the thought to work its way to completion: someone had tried to kill me.

Who?

Why?

Even after having my head banged around, I thought I had an idea about the second question. Whoever it was, they'd been coming from the same direction as me, which meant Astoria. I'd upset a number of people back there—Arlen and Neil came first to mind, but Jane and Candy hadn't been too happy either. None of them had liked me poking around, investigating Richard's death.

Which meant someone had tried to stop me.

Which meant someone didn't want me to learn what had really happened all those years ago.

It was one thing to know, logically, that the killer was still out there. It wasn't all that scary when it was nothing more than a logical conclusion—a theory, not a reality. It was quite another to have the, uh, rubber meet the road, so to speak.

But if the killer had run me off the road, why hadn't they stuck around to make sure the job was finished? Without my phone, and without the clock on the dash, I had no idea how much time had passed since the crash. Fifteen minutes? Half an hour? It didn't seem like it could have been any longer. Plenty of time for the killer to park and come to investigate, to make sure I was dead. But maybe the killer wasn't brave enough for a possible face-to-face confrontation. Or maybe they had seen the accident and thought there was no way I could have survived. (I was looking forward to surprising them on that particular point.) Or maybe they were waiting for some reason.

That was when I heard the first rock skitter down the slope. The sound was unmistakable. Another came a moment later—this one pinged off the side of the Jeep. And then a third. Ragged breathing and the unmistakable crunch of footsteps on scree told me this wasn't an animal. This was a person. And they were hurrying toward me as fast as they could.

I crouched down in the Jeep. Then I straightened again, trying to see out the window. No luck, of course, because the branches were in the way.

The sounds of frantic movement came closer.

Should I call out? If it were a passerby, or someone from emergency services, maybe I needed to let them know someone was still in here. But wouldn't they identify themselves? And if it was the killer—

I looked around for something to defend myself. The tire iron was in a storage compartment in the back, and it would take too long to retrieve. The first aid kit wasn't any use unless my attacker wanted a soothing facial with a disinfectant wipe. Maybe if I had a can of tire slime or something, I could blast him in the face, but, of course, I didn't. And then my eyes landed on the umbrella that had become an essential part of my gear since moving to the Pacific Northwest. It was compact, and it was cheap (because obviously I lost my umbrella almost constantly), but it was the spring-powered kind. So, when I pressed the little button on the side, the umbrella telescoped out and opened in a sudden burst.

It was better than nothing.

I retrieved the umbrella from where it had fallen in the accident, and then I perched on the center console, where I could launch myself up at the right moment. (God, please help me know when the right moment came.) The breathing sounded more labored now, and the rustle of weeds and the clumping, uneven steps sounded just outside. I still couldn't see anything. And then I could: the branches of pine on the driver's side window shifted, and the needles whispered. Whoever was coming, they still hadn't said anything, and that, more than anything else, told me I was in trouble. Any normal person—anyone who wasn't up to no good—would have called out, said something. Adrenaline boiled up from my gut. My face felt hot and slick. My headache seemed worse, in a way, but also far off, and I wondered again if I was going to be sick.

Above me, a gloved hand appeared. It was clutching a pistol, and it groped awkwardly, trying to get a grip on the window without losing hold of the gun. I didn't wait for an invitation; I leaped up from my perch, jabbed the umbrella between the branches in what I hoped was the right direction, and pressed the button. The umbrella shot out and connected with something that definitely wasn't a tree. The person outside the Jeep let go of the frame. The lodgepole shivered and skidded. The Jeep rocked slightly. And then there was a distinct thump as whoever had been trying to climb up to the window hit the ground.

The second surge of adrenaline caught me by surprise. I'd gotten them—whoever they were—good. I'd knocked them flat on their, uh, derrière. I had the upper hand. I needed to get out there, finish this while I still had a chance. I caught hold of the window frame and tried to pull myself up.

A gunshot cracked the air.

I let go of the window and dropped back into the Jeep.

The reality of my situation made its way through the fog of hormones. I wasn't winning. I didn't have the upper hand. I'd scored a tiny surprise. And the killer, on the other hand, had a gun—and I was trapped in a steel-and-fiberglass box. This was about as close as it got to literally shooting fish in a barrel.

I scooted toward the back of the Jeep, hoping I might be able to take cover behind the rock I'd hit, when a distant—and blessedly, belovedly familiar—voice rang out: "What's going on down there?"

Bobby was giving his deputy voice full steam.

From outside the Jeep came hurried movements, and then the snapping, crackling sounds of someone crashing through brush.

"HE'S GETTING AWAY!"

(Millie, of course.)

And then Indira said, "I think I can wing him."

"Put that down," Bobby ordered. "Keme, don't you dare run after him."

Even at the bottom of a hill, trapped in an overturned Jeep, I could hear Keme's sullen silence.

"If Dash is dead," Fox said, "do you think I can have those jeans he can't fit into anymore?"

"I'm not dead," I shouted. And somehow, I managed to climb up and poke my head out the window—the lodgepole had shifted just enough to give me clearance. They were all there, lined up on the side of the road. My family. And Bobby was practically running down the hill. "And what are you all doing here?"

CHAPTER 10

After Bobby and Keme hauled me out of the Jeep, I had to go through about eight performances of "Not that I'm not grateful."

"You didn't sound very grateful," Fox said.

"But I am."

"You sounded like that time Keme put a spider in your bath," Millie said.

"I—"

"And we drove all the way out here," Fox said.

"Yes, I know, but you were also kind of, um, vulturing my corpse, and I don't even think my jeans would fit you—" I caught myself a moment too late.

Fox froze me with a glare. "Not to wear," they said. "To burn. In your honor."

"Uh, right."

"After we drove all the way out here."

"That's enough," Indira said quietly. She had discreetly returned her gun to her enormous purse, but it was hard to forget the enthusiasm in her earlier offer to *wing him*.

"And again," I said, "I'm super grateful. I'm just not clear on why you *all* had to—ow!"

That was when Bobby apparently had reached his limit. He dragged me by the arm away from the rest of the group until we stood a good thirty yards farther up the shoulder. Then he released me so forcefully that it was almost a shove.

"Hey," I said.

But Bobby didn't say anything. The sun was setting, and it painted one side of him gold, highlighting the rich hue of his skin and the deep, earthy bronze of his eyes. The other side of him, though, it left in shadow. He had his hands on his hips, and it looked like that was more out of sheer force of will than anything—his fingertips were white from pressure, and he looked like a man holding himself together.

Somehow, though, he bit out two words: "What happened?"

I told him about my visit to Jane and Neil. I omitted—for the sake of expediency—my poking around Arlen's garage and workshop, but I did mention that someone had been watching me from his front window.

"And I know what you're going to ask," I said, "but it could have been any of them. Whoever it was, they were definitely pushing themselves—physically, I mean. But we're talking about a group of suspects who range from their sixties to their eighties. Neil is probably the fittest one, and even he would have been breathing hard by the time he got to the bottom of the hill."

Bobby didn't say anything for a moment. He looked like he was trying to take deep breaths, but instead, they were quick, and they sounded high in his chest. When he spoke, his words had a gasping quality that I'd never heard before. "I don't even have words." Breath. "For how stupid you are."

Headlights flared in the distance. The hum of tires, a long way off, moved toward us.

"Excuse me?" I said.

"You could have." Breath. "Gotten yourself killed."

I looked closer at him. Underneath the golden light of the sunset, he looked chalky, and his eyes were unusually wide. Beads of sweat glistened along his hairline and neck.

"Bobby—"

"You almost did." Breath. "Get yourself killed."

"Are you okay?"

"Because you did." Breath. "What I'm always telling you." Breath. "Not to do."

His hands left his hips, and he seemed to have lost track of them. One of them floated out at his side. The other he pressed to his chest before seeming to become aware of it again and pulling it away.

"I think you need to sit down—"

"You ran off on your own." Breath. "Like a child."

"I'm okay. Everything's okay, Bobby. I think you need to take a deep breath—"

"Everything is *not* okay!" His shout was strangely high pitched. "What if something happened to you?" And then his eyes got huge, and he pressed his hands to his chest and said in a normal tone, like we were having an ordinary conversation, "I think I'm having a heart attack."

"Dash?" Indira called from down the road.

"It's Bobby!" I shouted back. I got an arm under him to keep him from falling, which wasn't as easy as it sounds—Bobby is like 99% muscle, and I'm, well—what kind of paper do they make ice cream cartons out of?

The Last Picks hurried toward us as I lurched around, trying to keep Bobby (and me) from falling.

"What's wrong?" Indira asked.

"He said he was having a heart attack," Keme said. The boy was white with what I realized, a moment later, was fear.

"He's not having a heart attack," I said. My brain was starting to kick into gear after the shock. "He's in perfect health, he works out a ridiculous amount, and he doesn't even eat breakfast cookies or lunch cookies. He probably has the cholesterol levels of a stick of celery."

Bobby wasn't contributing much to the conversation at this point beyond the shrill, rapid breaths of hyperventilation.

"People in seemingly perfect health have cardiac events all the time," Indira said, pulling her phone from her purse. "I'm calling an ambulance."

"How long is that going to take?" Keme asked. His voice was so tight with worry that I almost didn't recognize it. "That's going to take too long. We should drive him." He looked like he tried to stop, but then he blurted, "We need to give him some Xanax."

That particular statement merited further investigation, I decided—I wanted to know what was happening, or had happened, in Keme's life that his first recourse was to dope someone up. But that was for later.

Millie looked equally at sea. "You should pat him on the back."

"He's not a newborn," I said.

"You should lay him on the ground and pump his legs," Fox said. Even they sounded a bit frazzled. "Get the bad air out of his system."

"I have no idea what that means," I said, "but it sounds like something from a spaghetti Western." Indira opened her mouth to say something, but I said, "Take it from someone who's had a baker's dozen of them: Bobby's having a panic attack."

Bobby moaned and shook his head, trying to say something.

"You're okay," I said. "I'm going to help him walk a little. He'll be all right in a few minutes."

"Dash—" Indira tried.

"You can call the ambulance if you want, but I think he'd rather talk to a doctor on his own. You know, privately."

She looked unhappy, but she didn't respond, and the phone stayed clutched at her side.

After a few final adjustments to make sure I could support Bobby's weight, I got us moving. We shuffled away from our friends. Bobby was still struggling to breathe. He was also still sweating. Like, a lot. Broken asphalt and loose stone crunched underfoot. The car I'd seen down the highway rushed past us, and the wall of air that rolled out behind it smelled like diesel exhaust and hot rubber.

Ahead of us, the sky was darkening to purple, and a line of cedars looked so perfect they might have been storybook illustrations.

After maybe a hundred yards, Bobby took a deeper breath, and the one after that was even deeper. He patted my arm, and I took that as a sign to stop. He leaned on me as he brought his breathing under control. Then, slowly, he covered his face with one hand.

He didn't need to tell me how hard this was for him—not just the physically awful experience of a panic attack (which, if you've never had one, actually does feel like a heart attack), but even more so, the loss of control. Because Bobby wanted so desperately to be in control. Not in a bad way, but in control of himself. Of his body. Of his emotions. And so, naturally, anything that made him lose control was terrifying. It felt like a lifetime ago when he'd told me that, when our relationship had been different, and he'd trusted me.

"Can I do something for you?" I asked.

He shook his head; he was still covering his face.

"Do you want some water?"

He shook his head again.

"Would it help if I had a panic attack too?"

He let out a noise that wasn't quite a laugh.

"Because I'm really good at them," I said. "Like, I might have the world record. One time I had a panic attack about having panic attacks. I think that's a meta-panic attack."

When Bobby spoke, his voice was rough. "I'm sorry about that."

"Why are you sorry?"

He didn't answer.

"You're human," I said. "Humans have emotions. They get overwhelmed. Sometimes, there's just a lot going on, and it ends up, you know, having an effect."

Bobby's nod was mechanical. He spoke in the low, measured tones of someone trying too hard to explain. "I haven't been sleeping. I haven't been getting enough sleep, I mean. The new apartment, the move, Kiefer—" He stopped, and it was a while before he tried again. "I shouldn't have yelled at you. I couldn't—I felt like I couldn't say anything, like I couldn't talk, and the harder I tried, the worse it got."

I eased away from him, making sure he could stay upright on his own. Then, facing him, I took his hand in mine and eased it away from his face. He had nice hands; that was one of the things I'd noticed about him early on. And his hands fit mine just right. That was another of those things I'd realized. I squeezed, and I waited until he looked at me. It was a strangely hangdog look, his head still down, his eyes wary, as though I might have been waiting for this moment of vulnerability to—what? Hurt him? Mock him?

With a smile, I said, "Welcome to Crazy Town. Population two."

Behind us, Fox shouted like someone at the end of their rope, "Because pumping their legs gets the bad air out! I don't have to explain science to you!"

"Uh, population six," I said.

Bobby's answering smile was wan, lusterless. Not the goofy grin I'd come to—

I almost said I'd come to love.

"I do think you should talk to a doctor," I said. "About not sleeping. And, if you want, about this. They can give you a prescription in case it happens again."

Bobby didn't say anything, but eventually, he nodded.

"And if you're stressed about stuff, Bobby, you know you can talk to me, right? I mean, I recognize that, uh, earlier today was not my best look. But you're my best friend. Of course I want to know what's going on in your life. I'm a very good sounding board. Plus it's a great, um, reason to take a break from writing."

He nodded again slowly.

"Oh, and we really need to figure out what's going on with Keme, because I don't like how quickly he jumped to prescription meds."

Bobby shook his head, a wavery movement that looked punch drunk more than anything, and managed to say, "Yeah, okay."

"Are you okay?" I asked.

He licked his lips. For a moment, I had the strangest sensation that he was about to say something. But then his expression changed, and all he did was nod.

"Want to be my bodyguard while we wait for a tow truck?" I asked.

He nodded. And, to my surprise, he held my hand all the way back to join the Last Picks.

Chapter 11

The next morning, I got up early and got to work.

Earlyish.

Okay, I *tried*. But it turned out, tumbling down a hill while strapped inside a couple of tons of metal and fiberglass takes a toll on the body. Every inch of me ached. My neck and shoulders were so stiff that I moved with the grace and poise of a young Frankenstein's monster. And the headache that had started last night had settled into what felt like permanent residency behind my eyes.

Eventually, though, I dragged myself into the bathroom. A hot shower helped. A longer, hotter soak in the tub helped even more. Best of all was the combo of acetaminophen and ibuprofen. By the time I was pulling on jeans and a tee (call me a pessimist, but this one just said GAME OVER and showed one of those ghosts from Pac-Man), I almost felt human.

As I made my way down to the kitchen, the sounds of my steps echoed back in the stillness of Hemlock House. Bobby had gone to work, of course, and Indira was probably at the farmer's market—I was fairly sure today was a Sunday. If Keme was around, he was probably in the billiard room slaughtering people on Xbox, but he might have gone surfing or to hang out with Millie or, as was often the case, simply disappeared, the way cats do, to do his secret Keme things.

Indira, bless her heart, had left me big, fat Belgian waffles, the ones with the sugar pearls, as well as fruit and whipped cream for toppings. I warmed up the waffles in the toaster (that's a life hack) and, uh, ate a reasonable amount. Look, there was fruit involved—take that, Bobby and everyone else who worries I'm going to get scurvy!

I was finishing my fifth (reasonable!) waffle when I made up my mind. Yes, I needed to do some writing with Hugo. Yes, I needed to do some of my own writing (I was more flexible on this point). But I couldn't stop thinking about the attack last night.

Because that was what it had been—someone (not an editor, not my parents, not Hugo) wanted me dead. Someone had tried to *kill* me. And although I wasn't everybody's cup of tea, I didn't regularly have people trying to end my life. At least, I hadn't before I moved to Hastings Rock. (Try not to act so surprised.) Which meant, as far as I was concerned, that whoever had tried to kill me had done so because I was looking into Richard's death.

That fact woke up the writer part of my brain. One of the necessary considerations for a cold case-style mystery was a reason for people in the present to care about a murder in the past. Often, it was easy enough to give someone a reason to want the investigation to succeed—a bereaved family member or friend wanted justice, etc. (Although, as my conversations with Vivienne's family had taught me, this wasn't, apparently, universally the case.) Slightly more difficult was creating reasons for people in the present to care about obstructing or ending an investigation. The easiest answer was that the killer was still alive and didn't want the truth to come out. The second one that came to mind was that someone was hiding a secret that wasn't necessarily about the killing, but that was somehow adjacent to it. Like, they'd done something they were ashamed of—or that maybe was illegal—and it might come to light in the course of the investigation.

So, what were we dealing with here?

And now that my writer brain was waking up, there were other pieces of this puzzle that I was trying to fit into place. When Bobby had asked me how sleuths in mystery novels solved cold cases, I'd told him about interviews, historical research, etc. And that was all true. But had I missed something? I ran through the examples that came to mind.

The easiest was, of course, the masterpiece: Agatha Christie's *Nemesis*. The book is stellar for a number of reasons. It's one of the later Miss Marple books, and by that point, Christie had honed her craft to perfection. Miss Marple isn't the cardboard cutout she is in the early books; she's grown and become more nuanced and complicated, and instead of being on the sidelines, offering advice to the police, she's now investigating crimes on her own. In fact, the premise of the book is so much better than just a cold case mystery (but it's Agatha Christie, so that's not a surprise). Miss Marple gets hired to investigate a crime—but she's not told what the crime is. Instead, she gets sent on a private tour, and, of course, she discovers not only the crime, but the killer. And, as usual, she does so through her usual combination of intuitive interviews and an intimate knowledge of human nature. But, since I wasn't particularly intuitive or incisive about human nature, I wasn't sure that example was going to help.

Another of the classics was Josephine Tey's Inspector Grant novel *The Daughter of Time*. This one was about as different from Christie as you could get. Police inspector Alan Grant, who has already successfully investigated other twisty mysteries in previous books, is laid up in hospital with a broken leg. In fact, he's confined to the hospital for the whole book. (Another coup, honestly.) Since he doesn't have anything better to do—because nobody had invented the internet, *Crime Cats*, or Xbox yet—he decides he's going to solve a mystery that's hundreds of years old: did Richard III kill the princes in the tower? (I guess if you're Josephine Tey, you play big or you go home.) He does the whole investigation from his bed by reading historical documents, interviewing physicians about the wounds and illnesses he finds in them, even by examining children's books. Super cool stuff, and a triumph of pushing the mystery genre to a new boundary, but it didn't give me anything new to work with. (Except, honestly, the idea of solving mysteries in bed. Maybe Bobby would have fewer objections if I took that approach? Or maybe Will Gower was, like, in a coma, but he could talk through some kind of brain-scanning-computer-thingy? I needed to work on the details.)

Vivienne herself had written a cold case mystery for her Matron of Murder series. It was darker than the Golden Age stuff, of course, like much of Vivienne's work. I couldn't remember the details, but it had to do with a married couple who turned out to be brother and sister. (And this was before *Game of Thrones!*) Oh, and they'd murdered their parents together. So, you know, that was a thing.

I toyed briefly with the idea that maybe the book had been based on a real experience, but Vivienne's father was very much (scarily) alive, and she certainly hadn't married her brother. Maybe there had been some taboo interest on her part? But even that didn't feel right—and Jane or Neil or Candy would have noticed.

Without anything better that came to mind, I decided I wanted to talk to Candy—without Arlen around to interrupt. I thought I had an idea how I might do that.

After loading my plate in the dishwasher, I ran up to my room (healed by the miracle of waffles) and grabbed a hoodie, my Mexico 66s, and my keys. Then I stopped because—oh yeah—the Jeep was currently in the possession of Mr. Del Real of Swift Lift Towing.

Well, shoot.

I took out my phone (which Mr. Del Real had returned to me after towing the Jeep away) and debated calling Millie. I didn't want to get her involved, but maybe she'd lend me her car—

"What do you think you're doing?"

I didn't *quite* jump out of my Mexico 66s, but it was close.

Keme, arms folded, glowered at me from the doorway. His dark hair was wet, and he wore his usual attire—a sun-faded and fraying Ripcurl tee, board shorts that were clearly a size too big for him, and his ancient, cracking slides. None of that, though, kept him from generating a surprising amount of menace.

"Jeez, you almost gave me a heart attack," I said. "What are you doing?"

"Keeping an eye on you so you don't do something stupid."

"Wait, how long have you—" I held up a finger. "In the first place, three of those waffles were defective."

Keme's expression didn't change much, but he did, somehow, manage to look disappointed in me.

"And second, what do you mean you're keeping an eye on me?"

"Bobby said—"

"What?"

(I might have lost control of my volume at that point.)

Keme must have realized he'd already said too much, though, because he just set his jaw and stared back at me.

"What exactly did Bobby say to you?"

He stared back at me.

"You realize this is completely inappropriate," I said. "He doesn't have any right to—to spy on me." I wanted to be mature enough to stop the rest of it, but it came spilling out. "Is this what he's going to do after he moves out? Have you tell him everything I do?"

For a moment, Keme's composure broke, baring the unhappiness that lay underneath. "Dash—"

"And what—if I go do something, you're going to follow me?"

Keme tightened his arms across his chest and looked away.

That confirmed my suspicion.

"You're going to call Bobby?" I asked, my voice rising again—disbelief mixing with outrage.

"He's worried about you," Keme mumbled. "He just wants to make sure you're okay."

"He needs to worry about himself because the next time I see him, I'm going to wring his neck." I took a deep breath. "Here's what's going to happen: you're going to go live your normal life like a normal teenage boy, and you're not going to spy on me because Bobby has an overdeveloped sense of responsibility. Meanwhile, I'm going to leave and go live my life independently and autonomously like an adult."

But when I stepped around Keme and started for the stairs, he trailed after me.

"Keme, I'm serious. Go play Xbox or scroll on TikTok or bother Millie at work."

He just stared at me.

When I turned for the stairs, he took a step after me.

"Keme!"

His face darkened, and he wouldn't meet my eyes, but he hunkered down like he was going to root himself in place if I tried to make him leave.

I opened my mouth, but before I could speak, Indira's voice floated up the stairs. "What's all the yelling about?"

Here's the thing about Indira. She's so smart. And composed. And calm. And mature. And all of those traits make me painfully self-conscious when I'm working myself up for a royal hissy fit.

I still managed to sound surprisingly petulant, though, when I said, "Bobby is making Keme spy on me. It's not necessary, and on top of that, it's not appropriate to put Keme in that position. And—" Genius struck. "—it's teaching Keme bad life lessons about, um, trust and relationships and stuff."

Admittedly, it lost some steam at the end, but I still thought I'd made a very good point.

Indira, though, only looked up at me from the bottom of the stairs. Then she called, "Keme, could you help Millie and Fox finish unloading the van?"

Keme glared at me—if looks could kill—as though this were somehow my fault. He stomped past me, which was pretty impressive in slides, and thundered down the stairs. A moment later, the front door banged shut, and then Indira and I were alone.

To my surprise, she came up the steps, her pace slow and measured. When she reached me, she asked, "How are you feeling?"

"Like the Jeep rolled on top of me."

A hint of a smile touched her face. She looked lovely today, of course. She always did—cream-colored trousers; a white top; a long, lightweight gray wrap that looked like the intersection of bathrobe and cardigan (in a good way). "Maybe you should take it easy today."

"I appreciate that, but I've got things to do." I struggled for a moment, and then the words burst out of me: "And I know Bobby is stressed about the move, and he's probably tied himself in a million knots about making everything perfect with Kiefer because, you know, he's Bobby, and he's not sleeping well, and he had that awful panic attack yesterday after we got in that argument—" As I listed all the things Bobby was dealing with right then, my anger started to melt. "—but this is crossing a line."

Indira listened. Then she was silent, and one of Hemlock House's very expensive clocks ticked away the seconds. Finally she said, "Bobby had a panic attack after you got in an argument."

"Yeah," I said. "He was super dysregulated, you know, no sleep, lots of stress, and then we fought and…" I couldn't read the look on her face. "What?"

She made a sound that might have meant anything. Then she said, "Bobby didn't ask Keme to spy on you. Bobby said he was worried about you. He was…upset last night, after you went to bed." And I got the feeling that *upset* wasn't the word Indira had originally been thinking. "Keme took it on himself to keep an eye on you. Because he loves you. And because he's worried about you too."

I mean, yes, at some level, I knew Keme and I were…attached, maybe? I don't know—whatever word you're supposed to use for your brother. Like, you can't get rid of them, and they steal your stuff all the time, and one time they gave you a dead leg that, like, *really* hurt. But the logical part of me, the part that understood this relationship, was having a hard time reconciling the words *love* and *worried* with the same boy who had, less than a week before, told Millie, *Watch this*, and then proceeded to strangle me with my own hoodie strings. (A surprisingly effective method of killing someone, I decided after I could breathe again. I was eager to have Will Gower try it on an annoying teenage hoodlum who ate all the snickerdoodles before he got any even though Will Gower had told him they were his favorite. Er, his favorite that week.)

"Frankly," Indira said, "we're all worried about you, Dash. This has become much more serious after yesterday's events. And we don't want you doing it alone."

"Okay, but if it's dangerous, then I don't want *you*—"

"This discussion is over now."

And she turned and went downstairs.

I was still kind of reeling as I followed her. Did that kind of thing always work? Or did it only work on me? Would it work if I tried it on Bobby the next time he started in on one of his lectures (lectures was a kind word, right?) about why I shouldn't crush up packets of Smarties and then blow the dust in Keme's hair?

(Keme had been so mad. It was amazing.)

When I got to the kitchen, Indira was directing Millie and Keme as they put away various baskets, display racks, and cake stands. Fox had found the rest of the whipped cream, and they were dipping Oreos in it. (Which, okay, was genius.)

"One time," Fox said, "I made out with a guy who had fallen off his motorcycle and then gotten run over by *another* motorcycle. Oh, and then a horse stepped on him." They gave me an unnecessarily pointed look, snapped off a bite of Oreo, and added, "Just saying."

"It's nice to see you too," I said. "Keme, I'm sorry. I shouldn't have gotten so worked up. It means a lot to me that you care—"

The boy had frozen as if transfixed, and his eyes were slowly widening in horror. He was even giving tiny, abortive shakes of his head.

"—uh," I fumbled for the rest of the sentence, but the best I could come up with was: "I love you too."

If you could have seen his face.

"And another time," Fox said, "I made out with a guy who had been kicked in the—" A polite cough. "—nuggets at the same time that someone blew an air horn in his ear." Another crisp bite of Oreo, and a pointed look for Keme. "Just saying."

"Fox, quit teasing them," Indira said.

"That was teasing?" I asked.

Keme was trying to assure Millie in a whisper, "I don't love him."

"Everyone focus," Indira said.

You'd better believe we all focused.

"We're going to help Dash with his investigation today so that Bobby can have some peace of mind," Indira said.

"That's sweet, but—" I tried.

"Not to mention keep Dash from getting himself killed," Fox said.

"That was less sweet. I really don't want you all risking—"

"There," Indira said. "That's settled."

And somehow, it was. Just like *This discussion is over now*. Would it work, I wanted to know, if I said it when I was trying to convince Bobby that no, three extra-large pizzas were not too much, on account of the miracle of leftovers?

"Fox, you're driving. Millie, you'll do research. Keme, you're going to watch Dash's back."

His little chest puffed right up. He ruined it, kind of, by checking to see if Millie had heard.

"And I'm bringing my gun," Indira said. "Now, Dashiell, where are we going?"

Chapter 12

My original thought was that I might catch Candy at work, but it turned out, the Neptune's Depths Seafood Processing plant was closed on Sundays (who'd have thunk?). So instead, we drove into Astoria.

It was another beautiful summer day, and Astoria was beautiful too. If you've never visited—or you've never seen *The Goonies* (shame on you)—it's not *actually* on the coast. It's a waterfront city, yes, but it's on the Columbia River. For over a hundred years, it's been a major port in the Pacific Northwest: timber, fur, import and export, commercial fishing, all that stuff. As in many port cities, there's a rift between the blue-collar workers who *do* the actual shipping and fishing and loading and unloading and processing, etc., and the business owners and managers and old-money families. So, for example, in addition to being a working port, Astoria also has a scenic river walk. It has tract homes, like the ones where Arlen, Candy, Neil, and Jane lived, but it also has big old Queen Annes up on the hill. (Side note: check out Airbnb. There's this one house where you can rent a room, and the room used to be the nursery, and there's this creepy old-timey bassinet in the room, and you have to *sleep* with that thing in there with you, and when Keme saw the pictures, he said it looked, quote, *haunted as*—well, a word that you can't put in an Airbnb listing). The Columbia River Bar (that's the spot where the river meets the ocean) is one of the most dangerous stretches of water in the world. Even huge commercial freighters occasionally capsize and go under there—no joke, not too long ago, it happened to a shipment of jeans, and people kept finding them washed up on the shore. In fact, it's so dangerous that, for years, it kept all those intrepid sailor-explorers from discovering the mouth of the river, even though they were sailing right in front of it.

In other words, Astoria was *not* Hastings Rock. It was beautiful in its own way, as I said, but it was a working city, a grittier city. The bumper sticker from Neil's truck came back to me: *We ain't quaint.* Hastings Rock was quaint. I had the feeling that if Astoria ever had a chance, it would give Hastings Rock an atomic wedgie and shove it in a locker.

We found the Skin Art Collective (excuse me while I throw up a little) in a strip mall on the outskirts of town. I say *we*, but it was really Millie—remember, she was on research duty. And honestly, there was something simultaneously endearing and satisfying about watching Fox try to keep their cool while the Maps app on Millie's phone announced, "At the next light, turn left," and then, a nanosecond later, Millie repeated, "AT THE NEXT LIGHT, TURN LEFT." It was hard to tell in the rearview mirror, but I thought Fox's eye was twitching.

The strip mall itself was a two-story brick building with big display windows on the ground floor and smaller windows above that suggested space originally meant to be residential. The Skin Art Collective occupied one of the end units, with a disturbing sign that showed a needle, thread, and skull. There was, less disturbingly, a dispensary (Rad Roots), a pipe store (Smoke & Barrel), a real estate office (Aspire Property Group), and a Chinese restaurant (Imperial Taste). The asphalt was worn and potholed, and weeds grew behind the parking stops. I wasn't sure what Aspire Property was aspiring to, but it probably included a sidewalk with fewer used needles and disposable contacts packages. Also, I know what you're thinking, and both Keme and I looked at Imperial Taste at the same time—but as soon as I opened the van door, the smell of rancid oil rolled over us, and we silently agreed to pass (this time).

I was halfway to the tattoo parlor when the sound of footsteps alerted me.

"Oh no," I said. "You're all staying in the van."

"Don't be ridiculous," Indira said. "We can't make sure you're safe if we're in the van."

"*I'm* being ridiculous? Indira, I'm going to confront this woman about, among other things, lying to me, and I'm going to try to get her to tell me where she was the night her brother disappeared, so I'm basically accusing her of murder. Also, I don't even have Bobby to distract her with his muscles and oh-so-vanilla sexiness."

I hadn't meant for that last part to slip out.

Millie beamed at me like I'd just earned a gold star.

Keme looked like he was trying not to throw up.

Fox choked on their spit.

Indira, patting Fox on the back, said, "All right. We'll wait outside."

"No, you can't just lurk on the sidewalk like a bunch of—" I managed to stop myself from saying *weirdos*, but maybe the message came through because Indira shot her eyebrows. "Uh," I said, "okay. Perfect."

"And Keme can go inside with you."

I opened my mouth to protest, but I realized this was a losing battle. And, all things considered, Keme was probably the best choice—he wouldn't talk much, unlike certain other people I could name, and if push came to shove, well, I mean, he *was* freakishly strong. (I still think Bobby lets him win at arm wrestling, but Bobby just gets that goofy smile when I ask.)

When we stepped inside, a bell jingled on the door, and music met us. I didn't recognize the song or the band, but it was metal, and it was, um, angry? The store seemed to be lit only by natural light, which meant no headache from annoying fluorescents but which, I thought, might turn out to be an inconvenience when it came to, oh, putting indelible lines of ink on the human body. Beyond a small waiting area with a counter and register was the tattoo parlor's studio space, with three different stations set up with tattoo chairs, rolling carts covered in supplies, and machines that looked like they'd been designed by someone whose true passion was torture. I mean, it's a needle going into your skin. Like, millions of times. Tell me I'm wrong.

Maybe Keme saw it on my face because he snorted.

At the back of the shop, Candy sat sidesaddle in one of the tattoo chairs. She'd lost the kimono today, and she was wearing a pair of poisonously green snakeskin boots, Daisy Dukes, and (rather optimistically, in my opinion) an ombre tube top that had probably been described as "tequila sunrise." She was talking to a man with stringy, graying hair. He wore a leather vest (no shirt underneath, of course), boot-cut jeans, and big, stompy-looking boots. The first smell I'd caught when I'd stepped into the tattoo parlor made me think of disinfectant, but now I caught a whiff of something else—a scent I occasionally noticed lingering around Fox.

"Can I help you?" the man asked, getting up from his seat. He was taller than I'd realized. Bigger too. I decided that, if necessary, today would be the day that I'd let Keme vent all that teenage aggression he'd been bottling up. Plus—bonus—Millie would get to watch.

"Uh, hi," I said. "I was looking for Candy."

"And who are you?"

"It's okay," I said, "I can see her right there. Hi, Candy."

Keme gave a little, subvocal groan.

"I asked you your name," the man said.

"It's okay, Ricky," Candy said and patted his arm. Then, her voice flat—almost hostile—she asked, "What?"

"I'm sorry to bother you, but I had a few more questions. I promise I'll be quick."

"Questions about what?" the man—Ricky—asked.

"Uh, tattoos?" I said.

Keme gave another of those little groans.

But it got worse a moment later when Candy's gaze slid past me, toward the big display windows, and she said, "Did you bring your mom?"

"Okay, wow—"

"And who's that? Your—"

Someone tapped on the glass in a way that could only be described as pugnacious, and then, their voice muffled as it passed through the window, Fox called, "I'm his titi."

"Oh my God," I said under my breath.

"AND I'M HIS SISTER!"

(No glass in the world could muffle *that* one.)

"Nope," I tried.

"And what are you?" Candy asked Keme.

"His big brother," Keme said without missing a beat. "I'm the one who wants the tattoo."

"He's not—" I began.

"Oh my God," Candy said, "I can totally see the resemblance!"

For a single, spluttering moment, there was only, um, spluttering. And then I said, "You can?"

"Candy said you're the best," Keme said to Ricky. "I'm thinking something minimalist. Maybe a scene from *John Wick*."

"Not one single thing about *John Wick* is minimalist," I began, "and you are *not* getting a—" But then I caught Keme's look (the translation was somewhere between *How stupid are you?* and one of those wordless noises of pure frustration), and I realized what he was doing. "Uh, okay. Maybe I could chat with Candy really quickly while you talk about it. And *only* talk about it."

Keme ignored me, of course, and pulled out his phone as he moved over to Ricky, apparently to show him what a minimalist tattoo of a scene from a *John Wick* movie might conceivably look like.

Candy stayed where she was, looking up at Ricky, clearly hoping to be included in the conversation—or at least acknowledged. But Ricky was, apparently, a true professional, and now that there was work at hand, he seemed to have forgotten Candy entirely. After a few more seconds, she heaved herself to her feet with a sigh and came over to me.

"What?" she said.

"Sorry about—"

"Oh, it's okay. I get it, trust me. Big brothers are the *worst*."

I almost—*almost*—descended into sputtering again. But I managed to keep my cool (on the outside, anyway—I mean was it the hair? He was seventeen, for heaven's sake. Was it because of all the testosterone?). "Right. Well, I was hoping I could ask you a few more questions about Richard."

She lowered turquoise-shadowed eyelids and squinted out at me. Slowly, she said, "Okay."

"One of the things that I'm still trying to figure out is where you were the night Richard disappeared." (I didn't add that the reason I was still trying to figure it out was because the first time I'd asked, she'd avoided the question.) "I was hoping you could tell me what you were doing that night."

Her silence lasted a beat. And then she said, "Excuse me?"

"This is part of making sure the case is airtight—"

"The case *is* airtight," she said, and the words were starting to get pitchy. "Vivienne killed him. I already told you that."

"I know, but you understand that to prove that, the police are going to need more than your word for it."

"I told you about all of it. How they were all fighting. And the money. She hated Richard, and she killed him, and she took the money and left."

"Yes, I remember you telling me. But you know that defense attorneys do background checks on everyone involved in a case like this—including witnesses. So, I need to nail down exactly where you were that night."

"I was at home." She said it so fast that nobody would have believed her.

"Uh huh. So, the thing is, another name came up in the investigation, and I'm afraid it's…complicating the timeline." (How about that for some grade-A BS?) "What can you tell me about Zane Potthof?"

Underneath the inches of makeup, her face went white. It was like someone ripped the stuffing out of her—her shoulders slumped, and she sagged inside her tube top (try not to visualize it). Then she rallied. She struggled to pull herself upright, crossed her arms under her, uh, bosom, and said, "Who told you about Zane?" And before I could say anything, she said, "It was *her*, wasn't it?"

"Who?"

"Of course she'd bring him up. Because that's how she is! She's always been such a dried-up old stick-in-the-mud. She's never made any mistakes. She's never done anything wrong. What did she say? What did she tell you?" Again, I didn't have a chance to speak before she barreled forward: "I don't care. I don't want to know!"

"Why don't we start with who you think—"

"Vivienne!" It was a shriek, and Keme and Ricky looked up from the book of tattoo designs they were examining.

A moment later, that combative tap came at the window, and Fox asked through the glass, "What did she say about Vivienne?"

That was when I decided that this would be the first—and last—episode of family-style sleuthing.

Fortunately, Candy was on a real tear by then, and she just kept going. "She's always hated us. She hates that we're her family, that she came from us, that she can't get rid of us. And she *hated* Richard. You said you wanted to know why she'd hurt him—*that's* why. She hated him so much she—she was insane. She would have done anything to hurt him."

"That doesn't make any sense," I said. "Everyone told us how close they were. Vivienne told us she loved Richard. Jane said—"

A nasty laugh ripped its way out of Candy, but she was crying too, wiping her cheeks and spreading mascara everywhere. "I *saw* them," she said, and the words had a child's outrage. "I walked *in* on them." And then, as though I might be even denser than she'd thought: "Doing it."

Maybe I was denser than she'd thought because the words that came out of my mouth were: "Vivienne and Richard?"

"No, you idiot. Vivienne and Jane! That's why Vivienne killed him. She was jealous of him! She hated him because she was obsessed with Jane. I told you Richard and Jane were arguing. I told you Jane was having an affair. Jeez, how dumb are you? She killed Richard to get him out of the way, made it look like a robbery, and—and threw Richard away like he was a piece of garbage." Candy let out that ugly laugh again, but now her eyes were dry. "Jane didn't want anything to do with her after that, though. Because she finally saw Vivienne for exactly who she was—who we all knew she was: someone who would do whatever it took to get what she wanted."

.

CHAPTER 13

Later that afternoon, surrounded by people on the beach, I was still trying to wrap my head around what Candy had told me.

After that revelation, I hadn't been able to get anything more out of Candy—she'd started crying so hard I thought she was going to make herself sick, and Ricky had asked us to leave. The ride back to Hastings Rock had been quiet. Too quiet, really, because I'd had too much time with my thoughts. And it hadn't gotten any better in the stillness of Hemlock House. I couldn't bring myself to check Bobby's room to see if he'd taken more of his stuff. I tried holing up in the den to work on my story with Hugo, but my brain seemed to have quit working. Hugo was understanding, of course. After an hour or two, he politely told me he needed to jump in the shower, and we'd work on it again tomorrow, and to have a great afternoon. Jump in the shower, I thought. On a Sunday afternoon. Which meant he was going out. Or maybe just hooking up with someone. And I was alone in a Class V haunted mansion while Bobby moved in with a baby gay fresh out of the packaging.

I heard how unkind that thought was and gave myself a stern talking to, but it didn't help.

Maybe that was why, when Fox told me to get in the van, I obeyed. I didn't even ask where we were going. And that was how I ended up at the beach, with so many other people that I thought I could actually feel my hair turning white, for the sandcastle competition.

It was *still* a beautiful day; maybe even more beautiful, in fact, on the water. The sky was the deep blue of a summer day winding to a close, with puffy white clouds marching along the horizon. Under the late afternoon sun, it was almost warm enough to feel hot, but the breeze and the swash of cold water kept it comfortable. When I looked out at the ocean, and the bright patches of reflected sunlight churning in the dark green water, I thought of silver-backed leaves turning over and over in the dark. I thought maybe I'd use that in a book one day. In a scene after someone died.

I tried to turn my brain toward the mystery I was supposed to be solving, but that didn't get me anywhere either. The revelation that Vivienne and Jane had been sexually involved—*if* it was true—changed the relationship dynamics underpinning the entire investigation. I knew, rationally, the revelation was important. I knew I needed to confirm it. But I felt braindead and hollowed out. When I tried to force myself to think, I came up with details that seemed useless—in Agatha Christie's *Nemesis*, the question of a same-sex desire underpins much of the story, but it's presented as obsessive and twisted. And Josephine Tey's biographers have long suggested that she was a closeted lesbian herself. Were those facts important? Or were they just my exhausted brain randomly firing in an attempt to make connections?

I had no idea, which was part of the problem.

A bigger part of the problem was that it was hard to focus on a mystery, or on feeling sorry for myself—or, frankly, on feeling melodramatic—with so much happening around me. People—tourists and locals alike—crowded the beach, and it seemed like they took up every inch of available space. Many of them had clearly been there all day, working on elaborate designs, and I realized with a hint of guilt that my friends probably would have been here too if they hadn't been making sure I didn't get myself killed. We finally found a spot a quarter mile down the beach and got ourselves set up. It wasn't a hard walk, and everybody besides me seemed to be in decent spirits. Keme was clearly thrilled about the opportunity to demonstrate for Millie his capacity for carrying heavy things.

I turned down Indira and Fox's invitation to help them with their sandcastle. (In case you're wondering—no, Keme did *not* offer, and I was going to remember that because his birthday was coming up.) I set to work on my own design, using the little trowels and scoops and buckets to excavate my raw material and then start building.

Even here, at the edge of the crowd, it wasn't exactly quiet. A little girl shouted with excitement as she sprinted toward the water. When the swash rolled up the beach, she came running back. It was, apparently, an endless game. Mr. Cheek, who had dressed in one of those full-body, old-timey bathing suits (the striped kind, you know?), was busy having an energetic discussion with an out-of-towner in an enormous sunhat. (He was telling her about his own, personal additions to the standard sandcastle design. I swear to God, I heard the word *bathhouse* about seven times.) Brad Newsum, of Newsum Decorative Rock, had marshaled what appeared to be an army of teenagers to create a sandcastle city. The teens—the boys, in particular—looked over at Keme a few times. They didn't say anything, though. And Keme pretended not to notice.

He actually might *not* have noticed because he was thoroughly engaged in some hardcore (and, frankly, agonizing to watch) teenage boy flirting. He stole Millie's hat, and she had to chase him to give it back. He knocked over the tower she was building, which turned into a splash war at the edge of the water. He had somehow (God bless that enterprising young man) managed to find a reason to take his shirt off, and he had apparently chosen as his latest act of, uh, courtship to bump into Millie as hard as he could every time she tried to add a detail to their design.

Fox and Indira, on the other hand, had what appeared to be a solid working relationship. Fox, who had worn a magenta caftan to the beach (the outfit was completed by foam beach slides that were designed to look like googly-eyed fish), was snoring softly as they napped. Indira's sandcastle was—let's face it—perfect. It had some strong *Sleeping Beauty* vibes, and there was something soothing about watching Indira at work: the concentration on her face, the steady, self-assured movements of her hands.

"Dash, your rock looks good," Millie said.

I stared at her. And then I looked back at my lump of a sandcastle.

Keme whispered something in Millie's ear, and Millie giggled before she clapped a hand over her mouth.

"It's not a rock," I said. "It's—I'm just getting started!"

"Why don't you help me, dear?" Indira asked. "You're so good at adding the little scallops."

Okay, I have to admit—that *almost* worked. Because I *was* very good at adding the little scallops. But I caught myself and said, "No, thanks. I'm going to keep working on my sandcastle."

Keme whispered something else, and that *really* cracked Millie up. She at least had the good grace to look guilty about it, though.

I was about to respond to that when an excited laugh broke through my thoughts.

Immediately to my right, no more than twenty yards away, Bobby and Kiefer had just arrived. Kiefer was on his feet, holding his hands up as though warding Bobby off, and grinning. Bobby, for his part, sat crisscross on the ground, shaking sand out of his shirt. To judge from the look on Kiefer's face, I knew who had put it there. And to judge by the look on Bobby's face—well, he was smiling. But it was clear Kiefer wanted to do some of the playful chasing I'd seen from Keme and Millie not too long ago, and it was equally clear Bobby had no intention of getting to his feet.

"Maybe you should come work over here," Indira said.

I shook my head and bent over my sandcastle—it was *not* a rock. And, just to prove my point, I shaved a bit off the sides to square it up. And then I added windows. And then because there was something soothing about poking my finger into the sand as hard as I could, over and over again, I got a little carried away, and the rock-castle crumbled.

"That's okay, Dash," Millie called brightly. "That happened to me all the time when I was little."

I chose not to respond to that.

The problem, though, was that now that I knew Bobby and Kiefer were nearby, I couldn't help but notice, well, everything.

"I just feel so bad for her, babe," Kiefer was saying. "I mean, she's so talented, and she's such a good person, and she totally didn't deserve that."

Bobby made a noncommittal noise in response. I recognized that noise. I had once, memorably, heard that noise when Bobby had been resting with his eyes closed and I'd ranked all the *Spider-Man* movies by gayness.

"I just don't know how she's ever going to perform again," Kiefer said.

Bobby's response came a moment later—polite, but distracted. "Who?"

"Ariana Grande," Kiefer said, with all the charmed vexation of someone who is deeply (and newly) in love. "The bombing. Remember?"

"Right," Bobby said in that same tone. "I don't know."

Kiefer gave an exaggerated sigh. Then, without missing a beat, he said, "Oh, remember how I told you Uggs were going to come back? Well, get this: they're totally coming back."

Bobby said, "Uh huh."

Okay, I'm a terrible person. I admit it. But at that moment, I couldn't help it—I turned my head down and focused on my sandcastle as I smiled.

At a generous guess, I'd say Bobby got about five seconds of precious silence before Kiefer said, "Oh my God, did you watch the clip I sent you?"

It might have been my imagination, but it sounded like Bobby's troweling was getting a little more...assertive. His voice sounded level, though, when he said, "I don't know. Which one?"

"Bobby!" But the mock disappointment vanished in excitement as Kiefer continued, "The one from *Watch What Happens Live.* You've got to watch it—I saw it last night, and I couldn't wait to show you." With that same callow attempt at weariness, he added, "That's why I sent it to you. It'll be so nice to just watch all the same shows once we move in together so I don't have to remind you to watch the clips I send you."

And there was a mind-boggler of a sentence, I thought.

Out of the corner of my eye, I could see Kiefer showing Bobby something on his phone. (Fine, I admit it: I was watching them.) I knew when the video ended because Kiefer looked at Bobby, clearly waiting for a reaction. Whatever he wanted, though, he wasn't getting, because finally he burst out, "Doesn't he look terrible?"

"I think Andy Cohen always looks like that."

"No, not Andy. Matthew Perry!"

For the first time, Kiefer's frustration seemed real rather than manufactured. They lapsed into silence. And because I'm a terrible person, I couldn't help but grin as I went back to work. I could even feel bad for Kiefer, a little. I mean, it was obvious he didn't know Bobby at all. Celebrity news? Fashion trends? Bravo TV? Getting Bobby Mai to talk—to really talk, not just those polite, noncommittal responses—was no mean feat, but as someone who was a master at it, I could tell that Kiefer had zero idea what he was doing.

And then, in the tone of someone clearly out of his depths but trying—as always—so earnestly, Bobby said, "I'm sorry. I don't know anything about that stuff. Matthew Perry was on *Friends*, right? Why does he look so bad?"

Between one heartbeat and the next, I couldn't breathe. It was like a big, brass hand had closed around my chest. Tears flooded my eyes, and even though I blinked as fast as I could, they spilled down my cheeks. I staggered to my feet, knocking over the rest of my sandcastle in the process, and lurched into the throng of people.

"Dash?" Millie called after me.

Indira said something I couldn't hear.

I was fairly sure Fox snorted themselves awake.

All of it registered at a distance, though. All I could focus on was that crushing sensation in my chest, and the sobs tearing through me, and the press of bodies, the hub of voices, the pounding beat of music—all that noise and heat and proximity, sharpening the edge of my anxiety until it was close to full-blown panic, and all I could do was run.

It turned out that, even on autopilot, my body knew what to do; somehow, I ended up sitting on a parking stop behind the food trucks. It wasn't exactly quiet, or even pleasant—the trucks' generators were loud, and the air was thick with exhaust—but it was blessedly free of people. The curb was pleasantly warm under me, and the sun was at my back. I put my head between my knees and cried.

More than anything, it was the surprise of it—that feeling of being caught off guard—that was the most terrifying. Until now, I'd been angry at Bobby. I'd been frustrated. Yes, I'd been hurt. But all those feelings had been, in their own way, buffers—safety mechanisms to cushion me from this. And *this*, now that it was here, was so huge and so awful and so painful, that for a few moments, I thought I was having a panic attack of my own: the tightness in my chest, the thickness of my throat, the animal part of my body screaming at me that I was dying.

But it passed. It always does. And then I just cried out of hurt and disappointment and loss.

I was still crying when the hinges squeaked. There was a step. Then a pause. And then a familiar voice said, "Who do this?"

Wiping my face, I shook my head, but I couldn't quite summon up words.

A moment later, Sergey crouched in front of me. The short-order cook for Let's Taco Bout Tacos had thinning blond hair cropped close to the scalp, pink cheeks, and the face shape (and muscles, and hairy forearms, etc.) of a villain out of *Die Hard*. He was also a very big Dashiell Dawson Dane fan, for reasons I didn't understand, although I suspected it had something to do with the fact that I single-handedly bought enough tacos to keep them in business.

Sergey stared at me for a moment. Then he patted me on the head. Not once, mind you—he just kept patting. And in a quietly terrifying voice, he asked again, "Who do this?"

"Nobody," I said—or tried to. There was a lot of sniffling. My eyes stung, and I was snotty from all the crying. "Nobody. Nothing happened." And it's probably hard to believe, but there was something weirdly comforting about having him pat my head, and I found myself struggling with tears again. "I'm so stupid. I'm such an idiot, and I ruined everything."

Pat. Pat. Pat.

Gently, Sergey said, "You no idiot. You number one boy."

"No. I'm *not* number one boy. I'm number one dummy."

"No," Sergey corrected—a little forcefully. So forcefully, in fact, that if there had been less head patting, I might have thought we were getting into an argument. "You no dummy. You bear."

I wiped my eyes and tried to get a fix on him. "Uh, not really. I mean, I'm not very hairy. Or big. Or snuggly. I'm not really into the whole tribe thing, but I guess if I had to pick, I'd be more of a—"

"No," Sergey said. "Some men like cock."

Ladies and gentlemen, you could have heard a pin drop. (Okay, not really, on account of the trucks and generators and seagulls.)

"What is happening with everyone's language?" I asked. "First Fox, now you. And yes, I mean, some men prefer, um, dudes, and other men prefer, uh, dudettes." Great. Now I was living inside a movie from the 1990s. (Why couldn't I think of one movie from the '90s off the top of my head? *Point Break!* But I wasn't sure they said *dudettes* in *Point Break*—)

I couldn't finish that line of thought because LaLeesha stepped out of the truck at that moment. LaLeesha is about half a foot taller than me, has the best skin I've ever seen, and spends a lot of time and money on her braids. She's a certified taco genius, and at that moment, she looked like a goddess descending to earth with a compostable takeout container in her hands. Inside the takeout container were three tacos. I swear I heard angels singing hallelujah.

"He means a rooster," explained LaLeesha. As she handed me the tacos, she continued, "And he's talking about traits. Some people are like roosters."

Sergey nodded as though this had all been rather obvious. "Some men like cock."

I still feel like I wasn't crazy for jumping to conclusions.

"You no like cock," Sergey told me.

LaLeesha's mouth twitched, and I sent her a dark look—which was, admittedly difficult when I was sinking my teeth into—

"Oh my God," I moaned around the taco. "Is that pineapple-mango *al pastor*?"

"You bear," Sergey told me. And he put his hand over my heart. (Which did kind of get in the way of my taco-eating.) "You heart of bear."

I paused mid-taco—mostly for air, but also to politely say, "Thank you, but I don't feel like I—"

"And you brain of mouse."

"Uh, because mice are resilient, I hope—"

LaLeesha didn't even try not to laugh.

Sergey was nodding, but it didn't seem to be about my rather optimistic interpretation. It seemed, instead, to be about something that had occurred to him. He was sitting back on his heels, considering me with a new look in his eyes. "And you body of hedgehog."

"Okay, but—seriously, Sergey? Body of hedgehog? What about body of, I don't know, deer? Deer are graceful. Or even, um, body of fox, I guess." Now I was getting into it. "Or body of meerkat!"

"Body of hedgehog," Sergey said, mostly as though in confirmation to himself.

"I liked heart of bear better."

"You heart of bear."

"I don't know—"

"You heart of bear."

There it was again—that tone like I'd better get on board, or things were going to get ugly.

"I guess I'm heart of bear."

He said more forcefully, "You heart of bear."

"I'm heart of bear."

More loudly again, "You heart of bear."

"I'm heart of bear!" I shouted (but not until I'd started in on the second taco, which—wait for it—was deep-fried Baja fish).

"Yes. And you number one boy."

"I *am* number one boy!"

(Number one at eating tacos, anyway.)

Sergey nodded. He patted my head again. And then he reached behind his back and pulled out an enormous knife and said, "Now, you tell Sergey: who do this?"

"Okay," LaLeesha said, "are we done here? Because I need my cook to stay out of prison."

"Uh, yeah. Thank you, Sergey. That was—you didn't have to do that."

He nodded, murmured, "Number one boy," apparently in approval, and let LaLeesha lead him back into the truck.

I sat on the parking stop and finished my tacos. (The third one was street corn chicken, which was incredible.) I felt...better. I mean, it was hard not to take the *body of hedgehog* thing personally, but I was going to assume it had been meant in the same spirit as the rest of Sergey's comments. Like, maybe I was good at protecting myself? (Hold your laughter, please.) Plus it was hard not to have your spirits lifted after having people take care of you—the yelling call-and-response thing had been weirdly rousing, and the tacos hadn't hurt either. I didn't let myself think about Bobby and Kiefer. I just sat there, enjoying the warmth of the sun, the sounds of the waves and happy voices, and this private haven that gave me a few minutes of peace away from all the peopling.

Two Girls and a Scoop (hands down, the best ice cream truck in Hastings Rock) was starting to call my name when my phone vibrated. Which, I guess, was someone *literally* calling me.

I didn't recognize the number, but I thought I had an idea this time what to expect.

"This call is originating at the Oregon State Penitentiary from," said a prerecorded voice. And then Vivienne said her name.

I accepted the call and said hello.

"I'd like an update," Vivienne said. "How is the investigation progressing?"

"Not well."

Her silence only lasted a beat. "What does that mean?"

"It means—" I stood and started down the boardwalk, moving away from the crowds and the rumbling generators. "—it's hard to conduct an effective investigation when the client lies to me."

"What in the world are you talking about? When did I lie to you?"

"Withholding information, Vivienne. That's lying by omission."

"Explain yourself."

"No, *you* explain yourself. I've spent the last few days trying to put together a story that's thirty years old, Vivienne, and being uncomfortably aware that everyone in your family seems to have a reason to lie to me. You didn't bother telling me that your ex-husband is still very much a part of the family. You didn't bother mentioning your little group of friends. You didn't tell me your ex had married Richard's widow, or that Jane was having an affair, or that nobody can account for Candy's whereabouts that night. You didn't tell me that someone would try to kill me, and let me tell you, I'm sick and tired—"

"What do you mean, someone tried to kill you? What happened?"

"Someone ran me off the road and then tried to finish the job with a gun."

"Are you all right?"

I ignored the question. "So, why don't we try this again: is there anything you want to tell me about Richard's disappearance? Anything you think I should know?"

The quality of the call wasn't great; in the background, the connection crackled, and static flared..

"You have got to be kidding me," I said.

"I don't know what you expect me to say."

"I don't know, Vivienne." I glanced around, cupped my hand around the phone, and whispered furiously, "How about, 'Yes, Jane was cheating on Richard, and it was with me.'"

Nothing. Into the silence of our conversation came the sounds of a city still busily alive: a family emerged from a shop down the street, the little girl talking excitedly about the kite she'd just gotten; Cyd Wofford zipped by on his bike and rang the bell in greeting; Althea Wilson roared around the corner in a boat of a Cadillac and nearly took out a newspaper box. (They were part of the tourist schtick, not real newspapers, although it was fun to see what Jemitha Green came up with every week.)

And then Vivienne made a faint sound.

"What does that mean?" I asked. "Is it true?"

"All this time," she said, "someone knew." She gave a strange laugh. "Who?"

"So, it is true."

Her voice gained strength. "Yes."

"And you didn't think that was important?"

"No, Dashiell—Dash. No, I didn't. Because it wasn't important. Jane wouldn't have killed Richard. She loved Richard."

"But she was sleeping with you."

"Yes."

But she didn't say anything else.

"Do you know what I should have asked you when you got me started on this idiotic search?" I said.

"Where was I the night Richard died?"

"That's right. What's your alibi, Vivienne? Because I've got to admit, Candy doesn't make a particularly compelling case—the nonsense about the money, about you leaving for Portland, your arguments with Richard. But when she told me about you and Jane, well, things started to take on a different light."

"I never would have hurt my brother."

"Everyone keeps telling me how much they loved Richard. Jane loved him, but she was sleeping with you. You loved him, but you were sleeping with his wife. Neil was his best friend, but now Neil's wearing Richard's jewelry and living in Richard's house and has basically taken over Richard's life. Hell, everyone tells me Neil is the son Arlen never had. Even Candy claims she loved Richard, but then it turns out she thinks he ruined her life. So, the problem, Vivienne, is that I'm not sure anyone loved Richard. He sounded like an unhappy, troubled man, who in the last year of his life was causing a lot of problems for the people around him. It's easy to talk about how much you love someone when he hasn't been around for the last thirty years to make your life more difficult."

I waited for the reaction—the denial, the insistence, maybe even the shouting. Instead, I thought I heard Vivienne swallow, and then she asked, "He's wearing Richard's jewelry?"

The question caught me off guard. "A bracelet," I said. "I saw it in the photo you sent me. Neil was wearing it the other day."

"I see." But her voice sounded numb.

I found myself suddenly adrift in the conversation—without the friction of her resistance to give it direction. After another silent moment, I tried to soften my voice. "Vivienne, I understand that you grew up in a different time. I know things weren't the same. But the world is different now, and whatever happened between you and Jane, it was a long time ago. You trusted me to try to find whoever killed your brother. For heaven's sake, *I'm* gay. Why wouldn't you tell me?"

"You're right." She cleared her throat, and a trace of her usual briskness came back into the words—but it was still only a pale imitation. "You're right, Dash. I should have told you. I apologize. I think—I think I've wasted your time."

"What do you mean?"

"I understand that you aren't willing to take their claims at face value," she said. "I understand that it's your role to be suspicious. But I promise you, neither Neil nor Jane killed Richard. Certainly not so that, years later, they could get married, and Neil could, as you put it, take over Richard's life. That's simply not what happened."

"With all due respect, Vivienne, I don't think there's any way you can know that."

"Yes," she said. "Well." And then she cleared her throat again. "I apologize again for not revealing the full extent of my relationship with Jane."

The pain in her voice, more than anything else, gave me pause. And there was something else too, a note I'd heard before, like she wasn't ready to stop talking.

So, I asked, "What happened?"

It was a broad question, and I meant—well, I wasn't sure exactly what I meant. Why did you both decide to marry men? Why did you have an affair? Why did it end?

Maybe Vivienne heard all of them. Maybe, after all those years of hiding, she simply wanted to talk.

"It was a different time," she said, and that familiar matter-of-factness I knew from watching her on television was blended now with something more human. "We knew about homosexuals, but not in any personal way. On top of that, there was far less discussion, shall we say, about how women were supposed to feel in a relationship. I loved Neil. And Jane loved Richard. They were both smart, athletic, handsome, and charming. It all seemed straightforward—we'd get married, Neil and Richard would get jobs, and we'd go on living the way we had been, as best friends."

I didn't say anything. The distant voices from the sandcastle competition competed with the crash of the surf.

"And then I actually *did* marry Neil, and…well, not to put too fine a point on it, but we discovered there was a long distance between a polite kiss on my father's porch and, well, the act itself. Neil did his best, of course, but I knew from that first night it wasn't going to work. We waited a respectable time, or what felt like a respectable time—we were children, so any time at all seemed like an eternity—and we divorced. My mother and father were furious, of course." She stopped. "Have you met my father?"

"In passing. Would it surprise you that he didn't want to talk?"

"Not particularly." Her hesitation suggested a silent struggle, and then she asked, "How is he?"

I thought about that. "Ornery. He threatened me with a shotgun the first time he saw me."

A bright, almost childlike laugh burst out of Vivienne. "That sounds like my father."

"Candy says Neil is more his son than Richard."

"By now, I imagine that's true. He took to Neil from the first time they met; Neil came over to study, and my father recognized him from the basketball team. They were a match made in heaven."

"Why was your father's relationship with Richard so strained?"

She laughed again, but it was colder this time. "No, Dash, I'm sorry. My father didn't kill my brother."

"Everyone talks about how charming Richard was. Why didn't it work on your father?"

"I suppose precisely because he *was* our father; parents tend to know us in a way no one else does. Richard and my father…they were like oil and water.

Once Richard became a teenager, they couldn't agree on anything. I'm sure you know how it is. Part of that was simply the son asserting himself, trying to establish his own identity. Rebellion against the authority figure of the father and all that. But part of it was personality; at some point, I believe, Richard decided to push back, and once Richard decided something, there was no changing his mind." Something about that tugged at the back of my mind—something about Richard, how he'd been fighting with everyone before he disappeared. But before I could try to follow up on the question, Vivienne continued, "Of course, it didn't help that our mother loved Richard so much."

"What do you mean?"

"Richard was the favorite. He could do no wrong. I'm barely a year younger, but you'd think I'd come from another family. Everything was Richard. It drove my father crazy, especially once he and Richard started fighting." Vivienne stopped, and then she broke her own silence unexpectedly. "The only time she ever fought with Richard was when he married Jane. I honestly thought my mother would rather kill him herself than see him in the hands of another woman. She never liked Jane; she thought Jane was putting on airs, which, if you know Jane, is the last thing Jane would do. It only got worse after the wedding. When Richard…went missing, my mother was already sick. She stopped speaking to Jane the moment she heard Richard had disappeared, and she never spoke to her again."

There was so much to follow up on, and I scrambled to pick the best question. "I heard Jane got cold feet before the wedding."

Vivienne measured breaths came across the call. "And you want to know if we were already involved."

"I don't know what I want to know. I'm just trying to understand. If she and Richard were already fighting, or if he did something—"

"Don't be ridiculous." She inhaled sharply, as though trying to rein in her temper. "No, Dash. Nothing happened. And no, we hadn't begun our…our affair, which simply sounds too tawdry. It began later. Neil and I were already divorced. One night, Jane came over. She was upset. Neil and Richard had been fighting." I could hear her struggling to master herself, trying to summon up that Matron of Murder matter-of-factness, but her voice quavered. "Had been brawling like teenagers, as a matter of fact. By that point, Richard was fighting with everyone, but it was most upsetting when it was with Neil, of course. She didn't want to go home. And I didn't want her to go home." For a moment, it was like Vivienne didn't remember she was speaking to me. "She had rain in her hair, and she smelled like camellias."

In the silence that came after, the sound of her painful, dry swallow came clearly across the phone's tiny speaker.

"Did Richard know?" I asked.

Waves slapped the sand. The afternoon sun laid a golden filigree over the surface of the water.

"Of course," she finally said.

Neither of us said anything for a while.

Something must have roused Vivienne, because she said in a poor attempt at briskness, "My time is up. I believe I've changed my mind. I no longer require your services, and I expect you to end your investigation immediately."

"What? Vivienne, they're going to hang this murder on you. Candy's story isn't all that great, but there's no alternative. Actually, that was one of the things I wanted to ask you about. When I asked her where she was that night, she lost her mind—"

"As I said, I no longer require your services." Vivienne continued in a gentler tone. "But since you are so hungry for alibis, allow me to put your mind at rest. I was with Candy the night my brother disappeared. She'd gotten herself into trouble. There was a man—"

"Zane Potthof?"

For a moment, Vivienne's surprise was audible in her pause. "Well done, Dash. Yes. Candy was infatuated with him. He was, among other things, a wastrel, a gambler, and a batterer of women. Richard had run him off once, to

Candy's dismay. Father hated him—I mean, my God, can you imagine?" Her voice turned mocking. "Arlen Lundgren, exalted leader of the Fraternal Order of the Sons of Sweden, Astoria Chapter, and his daughter is hooking up, I believe you'd say, with a man who was arrested the month before for public indecency. Candy went looking for Zane after Richard scared him away, of course; she's always been unhappy, and she's always been convinced that a man will solve her problems. She also, inconveniently, has terrible taste in men and doesn't have the common sense God gave a pair of shoes. I remember after the divorce watching her prance around Neil; I could have told her *that* wasn't going to work. Anyway, she'd gone after Zane, and he'd decided to soothe his wounded pride by taking his anger out on her, rather than facing Richard again. She called me from a pool hall across the state line, and I spent the night with her at a hospital. I *had* to go get her because if I didn't, Father would have tracked her down and killed her himself."

"But she made it sound like she was home when Jane came over."

"She was," Vivienne said. "I got her home a little before dawn. So, there you have it, Mr. Dane. Everyone has an alibi, and you can rest easy knowing you did your best on an impossible task."

Before she could disconnect, I blurted, "What happened with Jane?"

She was still there, still listening.

"Why did you leave? Why didn't you—I mean, you loved each other, didn't you?"

Her silence lasted so long that I began to think she wouldn't answer. But when she spoke, her voice was strangely gentle. "Allow me to tell you something you'd have learned on your own over time, Dash: love is never enough."

"What does that mean?"

Screams of excited laughter drifted down to me. Happy people living their happy lives. Birds cut the sky, nothing more than dark wings scissoring across the sunset. The waves kept coming.

"It means I was afraid." Vivienne's words were tight, the sound of someone trying their hardest to buckle down a sovereign emotion. "She wanted more. And I wanted to be famous."

CHAPTER 14

I couldn't go back to the sandcastle competition after that. Part of it was the disappointment of having been—well, fired wasn't the right word, since Vivienne hadn't been paying me. Dismissed, I guess. Pulled off the case. In an episode of *Law & Order*, Fox would have told me, I'd have been put on desk work, maybe even asked to turn in my badge and gun. It wasn't hard to tell why she'd done it; even now, Vivienne didn't want her secret getting out. It didn't matter that the world had changed. It didn't matter that, in a weird way, it might have actually helped her—she probably could have sold a lesbian book club version of the Matron of Murder series and made a mint.

The other part of what I felt was the heartbreak I'd heard in Vivienne's voice at the end. I didn't like Vivienne. In fact, I was downright scared of Vivienne. She was a murderer, and she was selfish, and she'd chosen to protect her own reputation over finding her brother's killer. But it was hard not to have a glimmer of sympathy for the everyday tragedy of her story—having to hide who she was, in a high school romance and then in an unhappy marriage and then in an affair with her brother's wife, and then, finally, in a life of solitude, wearing a mask she'd created for herself. The rational part of me knew that I shouldn't feel sorry for Vivienne; she wouldn't want me to feel sorry for her. She'd made her choices, and she'd chosen to gamble on herself, on her chance of becoming famous. She'd succeeded beyond her wildest dreams—and, of course, it had all come crashing down in the end.

But I also couldn't forget the girl I'd seen in the photograph Jane had shown me: young, innocent, happy. In love with her best friend. It wasn't even an uncommon story; maybe that's why it hit me so hard. When you were gay, same-sex friendships inevitably blurred the boundaries of attraction and desire—and even more so when you were an adolescent and first starting to understand that you might like boys, for example, in a way that not all boys did. I'd had it happen with Ben Michaelson, who, it turned out, did not appreciate having a Valentine delivered to his locker in seventh grade. It was why almost every gay kid has had the experience of being in love with a straight friend. Don't believe me? Do a quick search on Instagram.

Worst, though, were her words at the end: *Love is never enough.*

Those words followed me back to Hemlock House. It was dark and empty, full of long shadows and golden, glinting dusk. I put myself in the den and told myself to get to work. *The Next Night* wasn't going to finish itself. Hugo understood—and had a degree of patience for—my, um, idiosyncrasies, but the reality was that sooner or later, he was going to put his foot down. So, I pulled up the manuscript, scrolled to the scene I was supposed to be writing, and…stared at the page.

I'd left Hugo because I hadn't loved him—and, almost as important, because I'd been fairly sure he hadn't loved me. And I'd left because what I'd had with Hugo hadn't been enough. I'd wanted more. I'd wanted love. I wanted to love someone the way I thought it was supposed to feel—and that was part of the problem. I didn't know what it was supposed to feel like. I didn't know if love was even real. For all I knew, what I'd had with Hugo was as good as it got—someone to come home to, someone who cared about you, someone you had fun with. If there wasn't more—

I closed my eyes. I concentrated on my breathing. I counted slowly to ten, and then backward, until my heart slowed and the live wire of my anxiety was buried again. And then, keeping those thoughts at bay, I turned my attention to *The Next Night* and made myself start typing.

This scene was supposed to be one of the most important in the book. Dexter Drake, our intrepid investigator, was hiding in the bushes of Pershing Square, watching as his lover, Dan Garrett, was led away by police. Pershing Square was an infamous cruising spot for gay men in Los Angeles, and in the 1940s, when our book was set, it anchored The Run, a corridor of businesses that were gay friendly. Unfortunately, the popularity of the area also made it a frequent target of police officers—and civilians—who wanted to catch men in the act, so to speak. Now, as Dexter watched the police lead his lover away, he had a choice to make: try to save Dan, or make his escape—and let it happen again.

That *again* was the crucial part. Because *The Next Night* was a story about cycles, about bad things coming back around. Dexter's bad decisions with his lovers, of course (that was a noir staple). His bad life choices in general, actually—too much whiskey, too many gin joints, too much loneliness and grief that built and built until the pressure forced him to do something rash. (Another noir staple.) And, of course, the murders. A serial killer was operating along The Run, and the police were ignoring the murders of gay men and other marginalized people, which left only Dexter to try to stop him. But because this was noir, Dexter kept trying to fix things the way he always had. And so, nothing he tried ever worked. Which meant the next night, and the next, and the next, were always the same.

I hated it.

I stopped, hands above the keyboard. I'd never put it into words like that, but I *hated* the premise. I mean, it was good—Hugo's ideas were always good. It captured how the best noir mixed cynicism and despair with a refusal to surrender virtue, to continue to try to do good. Even though I knew I was too close to the project to be objective, I had enough awareness to know that it was sharp, incisive, powerful. Maybe even brilliant, because Hugo, according to all his starred reviews, was brilliant.

But as I sat there, staring at the keyboard, my stomach turned. I didn't *want* Dexter Drake to let the police drag Dan away. I didn't *want* Dexter to keep making the same bad choices, to go on living the same claustrophobic, hopeless life. Yes, it was historically accurate. Yes, it was true to the genre. Yes, it was a powerful and compelling tragedy, and it showed a sliver of what it might have meant to be gay in 1940s LA.

But what I wanted to do was send Will Gower in with his .38. He'd fire off a few warning shots, and the police would run for cover, and in the chaos, Will would get Dexter and Dan (God, I even hated that they both had names that started with D) to a private airfield, and they'd fly to Mexico. And Will Gower would find the serial killer, and Dexter and Dan would open a little hotel on the beach, and The End.

The story, which had seemed electric when Hugo and I had been brainstorming, felt dead now—limp, cumbersome, cold.

Why?

I tried to be rational about it. What had changed? I mean, it hadn't *only* been Hugo's idea. I'd been part of it too. I'd even been excited about it. But now, when I thought about writing that scene—about having Dexter watch his life fall apart again because he kept trying to solve his problems the same way, because he didn't know how to break the cycle—cold sweat dampened my tee, and little black spots whirled in my vision.

No answer came to me. Nothing I could put into words, anyway. Just my anxiety building in my chest until I finally set the laptop aside, pulled my favorite blanket over me, and lay back to concentrate on my breathing.

It's called meditation, for your information.

I knew it was a dream even while it was happening; lucid dreaming, I believe it's called. I was in the dark, in the brush and brambles of Pershing Square. But I wasn't Dexter Drake. Or maybe I was, but I was also Vivienne

Carver, and I was watching the police drag Jane away. Police lights flashed and spun. I wanted to shout. I wanted to move. But that particular paralysis of dreams held me, kept my throat shut, and I knew they were taking her away, and I'd never get her back. She was getting smaller and smaller, farther and farther away from me. And then a gunshot—

I jerked awake. I was hot under the blanket, and dizzy, but my sweat was the clammy sweat of a nightmare. Kicking the blanket off me, I sat up, gulping in air. The house was dark, and the only light in the den came from the lamp next to me. How long had I been aslee—uh, meditating?

My phone said it was almost eight, which seemed impossible. The dream had been so short.

The sounds of movement came from upstairs, and I froze. My brain began to piece together items from my lucid dreaming: the police lights flashing might have been headlights sweeping across the den's window, and the gunshot must have been a door closing. For another moment, I listened to the footsteps overhead. Then I got to my feet and went to investigate.

I didn't bother turning on any lights. In my stockinged feet, my steps made less than a whisper on the thick rugs. When I reached the second-floor landing, I could see the light under Bobby's door. What were the odds the killer had come after me, determined to finish the job, and walked right past me in the den in order to rummage around in Bobby's room?

Pretty low, I decided.

Bracing myself for another encounter with Kiefer, I rapped on the door. Be nice, I told myself. Smile. He's Bobby's friend, so you're going to figure out how to make things work, even if he wants to talk about—what did young people want to talk about? Music, I decided. Even if he wants to talk about, um, Hannah Montana. Wait, would Kiefer even know who Hannah Montana was? Maybe I should go back to my room, do some research on my phone, find out what the cool kids are talking about these days. Heck, I could even wait for Keme to get back—

"Yeah?" Bobby called, and the sounds of movement continued.

For about five seconds, I thought about running away. No plans. No luggage. Just me, possibly a bindle—

The door swung open, and Bobby stood there. It took a moment for my eyes to adjust to the light, but I knew his silhouette, knew what it felt like to be near him, knew how he took up space, the sounds he made that were just his body existing in the universe. Then I could see him. He was still dressed in his cute little number from earlier today: the white tank, the black shorts. He'd changed into sneakers—not any of the expensive ones he collected, but workhorse New Balances that he used when he needed a pair he didn't mind getting dirty. (Well, not too dirty. I mean, he still cleaned off all the scuffs.) The outfit left a lot of Bobby to look at. A lot of golden skin. A lot of muscles. And the way he was standing, arms folded, did, um, things, to his arms. And his chest. And his shoulders. And did you know a neck can be, like, veiny and weirdly strong and suddenly you think you might have a thing for necks? I heard the direction my thoughts were taking and decided the only safe spot to look at was his ear. (I mean, my God, have you seen his eyes?)

"I thought you were asleep," Bobby said. And then, "I woke you up."

"It's okay. I was having a bad dream. Also, as soon as I said that, I realized it made me sound like I was five years old, and I want to retract it. Wait, let me start over. I heard an intruder, and I came up here to beat him up."

He didn't exactly smile, but he did cock his head. "Are you okay?"

"Oh great. I mean, kind of facing crippling uncertainty about this stupid story with Hugo, and doubting all my artistic instincts and, you know, my life choices in general, and operating at about a 9.7 on the Barkhausen scale."

Bobby said, "What?"

"It's a scale I made up to measure my anxiety by how much I want to scream into my pillow. This little interaction just bumped me up to a 9.9, in case you're wondering." Since that didn't leave Bobby much room in the way of a response,

I decided to just jump into the rest of it. "I, uh, wanted to check on you. I mean, not right now. Because I thought you were an intruder."

"And you were going to fight me."

"Beat you up," I corrected. "But, you know, in general I wanted to check on you."

He didn't say anything.

"About the other day," I said.

He still didn't say anything.

"When, you, um—" *Had a panic attack* felt like too much, so I finished. "—you know, when the Jeep rolled."

"When you were forced off the road and almost killed," Bobby said.

"That."

"I'm fine." It seemed to cost him something to add, "Thank you for asking."

"Oh good. Great. That's—that's awesome sauce."

Bobby wasn't the eye-rolling type. But I could sense some emotions trying to make their way to the surface.

"So, like, what did the doctor say?"

More slowly, Bobby said, "I'm fine, Dash. I appreciate the concern. It was a one-time thing."

"Is that what the doctor said?"

"I've got it under control." He put his hand on the door, the nonverbal equivalent of: *I'm going to shut this now, so go away.* "I need to get back to work."

A year ago, I probably would have slunk away. Maybe even six months ago, because everything with Bobby had felt so precarious after Christmas. But a lot had changed in the last year. A lot had changed since Christmas. A lot, it turned out, had changed in the last month. And all of a sudden, I was angry.

"Great," I said, pushing past him into his room. "Let me help."

Aside from the cardboard boxes, most of which were taped and ready to go, the room looked like it always did—which was to say, like Bobby didn't live there. He was so neat. So organized. So considerate. Everything was always put away and in its place. Even with boxes all over the place, it felt more like a hotel room than somewhere someone actually lived. I had a vision of this room after all those boxes were gone, and it would be like every other room in Hemlock House. Frozen in time. A museum. Empty.

"So, did the doctor give you some exercises?" I asked. "Did you get a Xanax prescription in case it happens again? What did they say about seeing a therapist?"

Bobby turned to follow me as I moved around the room. He folded his arms again. He set his jaw. "What is this?"

"What do you mean?"

"What do you think you're doing?"

"I'm being your friend. I'm checking in."

"Really? Because it feels like you're trying to pick a fight."

"What would I be trying to pick a fight about?"

Bobby took a long breath through his nose. In tones so measured that they were like a klaxon for an imminent explosion, he said, "I didn't see a doctor."

"Oh! See, that was confusing because you kept answering my questions like you had. Kind of, you know, like you were lying to me."

"I wasn't lying to you. I was telling you the truth. I'm fine. Everything's fine. I have it under control." He seemed to think I needed further clarification, so he added, "I don't need to see a doctor."

I said something that would have gotten me kicked out of the sandcastle competition *tout de suite*.

Bobby said, "I need to finish packing."

"You've got it under control?" I said.

He stared at me a moment longer. Then he crossed the room, opened a dresser drawer, and took out a stack of clothes. Normally, Bobby moved with an unthinking grace; he was a natural athlete, and he was a surfer, and he moved like someone confident in his own body. Now, his movements were choppy. His back was stiff. He looked like his head might snap off his neck if he turned too quickly.

"Let's see," I said. "Like you had everything under control after you broke up with West."

He took out another stack of clothes.

"Remember that? When you were working every shift the sheriff would give you? And when you weren't working, you were going to the gym? And when you weren't at the gym, you were surfing—" My voice threatened to crack, so instead, I turned the volume up—anger instead of, you know, real feelings. (That's a life hack.) "—and almost getting yourself killed because it was stupid to be out there by yourself, stupid to be out there in that weather, stupid to be taking risks like that when you know better." Somehow, I managed to bring my voice down, although it stayed quavery. "Under control like that?"

A flush climbed Bobby's neck, rising into his cheeks. He looked away.

"You're not going to say anything?" I asked.

"What do you want me to say?"

And his quietness, his reserve, the wall between us that had never been there before—it reminded me of the conversations I'd overheard between Bobby and West. West's almost-shrewish complaining. Bobby's mild answers.

It made me go insane.

There's no other word for it. I can't defend or justify or excuse what happened next.

My volume rose with each word until I was shouting: "I want you to say that you're making a mistake!"

He still wouldn't look at me. He stood there, breathing slowly. And then he said, "I'm sorry you feel that way," and he turned and picked up another box.

"That's it?" A tiny voice at the back of my head told me to get myself under control, but it was too late for that. "You're sorry I feel that way? Because the subtext there is *screw you.*"

He was transferring some of the clothes he'd taken from the dresser to the box. He dropped the rest of them in, straightened, and turned to face me. The color was high in his cheeks now. "I don't know what you want me to say. I'm moving in with Kiefer because I love him—"

"You don't love him! You don't even know him!"

"You're my friend, but this conversation isn't productive—"

"No, this conversation is scary to you because I'm acting like a crazy person. Because my feelings are all out of whack. And your feelings are all out of whack, and you don't like that at all. You'll do just about anything so that you don't have to feel out of control."

For a moment, he was motionless. I wasn't even sure he was breathing. He stared back at me, but it wasn't like he was seeing me. Then, his voice gravelly, he said, "Fine. I'll come back when we've both cooled down—"

I moved into his path. "That's why you were trying to kill yourself with work and exercise and surfing after the breakup. That's why you're rushing into this thing with Kiefer, because you feel like your life is out of control, and he's twenty years old and he'll do whatever you want him to do, even if it means you're making a huge mistake because you don't want to live with him, and you certainly don't love him, you just want not to feel like this anymore."

"You had your chance!" The few times in my life I'd heard Bobby yell, it had been terrifying. This was no exception. Part of it was the sheer volume—he had a set of lungs on him—but most of it was watching his control snap. His cheeks were hectic, and he was breathing so hard he was almost hyperventilating. "I tried, Dash. I did everything I could to let you know how I felt about you, and you knew what I was doing. You *knew*." The hurt brought his voice to the edge of cracking. "And you found a million ways to tell me no without ever telling me no. So, you had your chance. I don't want to be alone forever. I don't want to—to wait, and to hope that someday, when you finally think I'm worth taking a risk for, you'll be open to the possibility of actually going out on a date. Nobody wants to live like that. You don't even want to live like that. But you're so scared that you won't even try, and I'm sorry about that because I want you to be happy." He wiped his eyes. His next words trembled as he tried to control himself. "I'm not going to be locked into this weird limbo, where you get all the benefits of a relationship without having to take any of the risks, just because you're scared. That's not fair to me. It's not fair to anyone."

There was simply too much in those words to process. Too much, and all of it too frightening, so I latched on to the part I could wrap my head around. "You knew I was bad at relationships. You knew I was scared. And you kept pushing and pushing because you don't like uncertainty, and you didn't want to wait."

"I pushed because I wanted to be with you."

"And I didn't want to be your rebound! You'd broken up with West, like, three months before that. You were still working through all of that. And I didn't want to jump into a relationship either—a year ago, I changed *everything*, Bobby, and that included leaving the only serious relationship I'd ever been in. Did you even think about the fact that I needed time too?"

"You told me to date other people. You told me you were going to be single forever. That you wanted to be single."

"Because I wanted both of us to have time to build a solid foundation for our relationship!"

"Are you insane?" Bobby shouted. "This isn't a story, Dash. You can't plot out people's lives and expect them to play along. I'm not a character in a book! I'm a person! I have feelings!"

"I have feelings too! And if you knew I was so scared, why couldn't you just come out and tell me what you wanted? Why couldn't you just say to my face that you liked me and that you wanted to try dating?"

Bobby was drawing harsh, long breaths through his nose. When he spoke, I didn't recognize his voice, but the words were clear. "All right. How's this for communication: I want to date you. What do you want?"

My throat closed up. One second became five. Five became ten. My eyes welled with tears, and I had to look away.

"This is why I'm moving in with Kiefer," Bobby said. "Because you still can't tell me how you feel."

I stood there, blinking to clear my eyes. I couldn't think. I couldn't come up with words. It was like my nightmare: paralysis of body and thought, unable to move or speak or even think. But then I saw, next to the lamp, his keys. I grabbed them.

"What do you think you're doing?" Bobby asked.

"I'm not letting you move in with him," I said and ran for the door.

Chapter 15

I sprinted through the dark house, clutching Bobby's keys. If he chased me, I didn't hear him—I couldn't hear anything over the hammer of my steps and my ragged breaths. A moment later, I was bursting out into the pleasant cool of an evening on the Oregon coast, the air sweet with hemlock and timothy and cedar and the brine of the sea. I climbed into the Pilot and started the car, and I sped down the drive. Then I was driving north, into the fog belt and the forest of spruce and fir and fern, where the trees rippled and whispered like a darker ocean.

I didn't have a plan. I wasn't even thinking, really. I'd gone into flight mode, and the higher-level functioning of my brain had completely shut down. But as the cocktail of hormones ebbed, clarity started to return. I couldn't go far. I was technically committing grand theft auto, for one reason. And, for another, where would I go? Back to my parents? Was I legally required to move after—well, whatever you called that scene back at Hemlock House? A farce? A travesty? A debacle?

A fight. A horribly, ugly fight with my best friend.

I want you to be happy.

I knew if I let myself think too much about what Bobby had said—what we had both said—I'd fall apart again, so I forced myself to take deep breaths, to let my thoughts slide away. They were leaves on a river, carried away by the water. They were cars on a road, zipping past me. They were, uh, pages in a book? I kept falling asleep during the meditation app, but there was probably another good metaphor in there somewhere.

By the time I pulled into the Hastings Rock Public Library's parking lot, I could have passed for a human being (if you didn't look too closely). I sat there for a while, my hands shaking until I clasped them in my lap. I let my head fall back. I closed my eyes. As the adrenaline leached out of my body, exhaustion took its place, accompanied by a renewed awareness of every ache and pang from the prior day's accident. I couldn't fall asleep. I had to work up the courage to drive back to Hemlock House. I'd leave the keys under the doormat, the way they did in movies sometimes. And I'd write a quitclaim deed leaving the house to Indira. And then I'd wander off into the forest and get eaten by a bear. Like that guy in that movie who got eaten by a bear.

Or, God help me, I could try—*try*—apologizing to Bobby.

But what would I say? Yes, I'm in love with you. You make me happy every day. I want to spend every minute I can with you. You're smart, and you're funny (but not too funny, like, in an annoying way), and you're so good with Keme that sometimes I think you have a built-in dad mode that got activated when you were twelve. You move your head when you listen to music, sometimes. You keep time with your fingers on your chest. You have this way of being in a place, in a space, like you have your own gravity, and even though every other hour of the day I feel like the ground is crumbling beneath me, when I'm around you, it's like I'm standing on something solid, and everything makes sense. So, yes, I want to spend the rest of my life listening to you explain why I can't park there because it's a red curb—

Someone tapped on the window.

I screamed.

Someone else screamed.

Somehow, I managed to crawl back inside my own skin and turn to look out of the Pilot.

Mrs. Shufflebottom stood there. Hastings Rock's head librarian had white hair, piercing eyes, and cardigans so disturbingly tight that they looked like straitjackets. (Like, you have no idea. It looked like she was vacuum sealed inside those things.) She was a heck of a librarian, from what I could tell—I was a regular patron, and the library had an impressive collection—and she did a fantastic Mrs. Claus at Christmas. She was also my self-proclaimed nemesis, and right then, she was staring at me through the window like she wanted to brain me, clutching her cardigan at her throat.

"Oh my God," I said. "I'm so—" I buzzed down the window. "I'm so sorry. You startled me."

To my surprise, Mrs. Shufflebottom gave a little laugh, and her chokehold on the cardigan relaxed. "And *you* startled *me*, Dashiell." I opened my mouth to correct her, but there was something strangely pleasant about how she said my full name. "You're parked in front of—" But then she stopped. "Are you all right?"

"Yeah, thanks."

It wasn't super convincing, though, because I started to cry. Not sobs. Not even tears running down my face. But my eyes stung, and I dropped my head.

Mrs. Shufflebottom made a soft noise. She patted my shoulder and said, "It's okay. It's okay. It's all going to be okay." I wasn't sure how—witchcraft, maybe—but somehow she got the Pilot's door open, and the next thing I knew, she was urging me out of the car. "Come inside and have some tea."

About my only coherent thought was to hope that, since she was my nemesis and all, it would be poisoned tea. Maybe she'd bury me under the library. Maybe I could be a not-so-friendly ghost haunting the cookbook section.

The library wasn't much to look at. It was a single-story brown building with a utilitarian design at odds with the rest of Hastings Rock's picturesque charm. Inside, it smelled like well-used carpet, aging paper, and the damp that settles into cloth and wood but that isn't quite mildew. The fluorescents were bright, but the acoustic tiles were water stained, and the windows were small and made the library feel unexpectedly close.

Still, Mrs. Shufflebottom had done her best. As I said, it had a first-rate collection, and although the furniture was mismatched, it was clear that she'd purchased items in an attempt to maximize comfort and usability (and frankly, cleanability—you'd be surprised at the kind of stuff people get up to in a library). (Not that. Get your mind out of the gutter.) She settled me in a plush armchair near the circulation desk and left me. I could hear her bustling around in the staff-only area. Before long, she came back with a tea service. This was the second time in the last week someone had brought me a tea service. I wasn't much of a tea drinker, but it made me feel so civilized.

After pouring the tea and offering me milk and sugar, Mrs. Shufflebottom seemed content to sit in silence as we drank. The mug was pleasantly warm between my hands, and although I wasn't a tea connoisseur, it tasted good. Some of the knots in my body untied themselves. Another wave of emotion washed over me, but it was gentler this time. Disappointment. Loss. Grief. I dabbed at my eyes with one of the little paper napkins and breathed my way through it.

Mrs. Shufflebottom patted my knee. "Do you want to talk about it?"

I shook my head.

"Shall I call someone for you?"

"No," I managed to croak. "Thank you." And then—because even in the depths of despair I was still, unmistakably, Dashiell Dawson Dane—I blurted, "Why are you being so nice to me?"

She patted my knee again, but she didn't answer for what felt like a long time. "I believe we got off to a bad start, Dashiell. I'm not happy about that. When you arrived, the circumstances with Vivienne, and then, of course, that scene with Pippi—" She took a breath and set her mug down. It clinked against the tray. She clasped her hands. "I believe I am a fair person, and I'd have to be blind not to see the good that you've done for people in this town." She held up a hand when I opened my mouth. "I don't only mean the murders, young man.

You've been a good friend to people whom this community has not always treated well. You're kind and respectful. You're a library card holder, and that goes a long way with me." It took me a moment to realize she was making a joke, and a crooked grin slipped out of me. She offered a small smile back. "And I was also very impressed that you didn't object or explain about the books. You simply paid the fine and went on with your day, even though someone else might have taken the time to explain that Keme had been the one who made you spill the hot chocolate."

I wasn't sure that anybody got so worked up about library fines that they had to blame a teenager, but then I said, "Wait—"

"Millie told me," Mrs. Shufflebottom said with another of those small smiles. "Your friends think very highly of you." After a quiet moment, she said, "I would like to apologize. I hope that I can be a better librarian to you in the future."

"You don't need to apologize. I mean, thank you. This is all—you're being very kind." My emotions were unraveling again. I grabbed some more of the napkins, wadded them against my face, and waved blindly at the tray. "You didn't have to do this."

"But I wanted to," Mrs. Shufflebottom said. And then, in a tone I could only call strained, she said, "And I certainly couldn't stay angry with a young man who was willing to help Vivienne Carver. I know what she did, and I know what it means, but—but she was important to me, and to this town, for a long time. She was my friend. Is my friend, I suppose. And when you're my age, I don't know how to explain it—I certainly don't condone her behavior, but perhaps, in a way, I understand it." She rose, waving for me to stay in my seat. "I'm trying to say I'm thankful. I know you didn't have to help her. I'd like to show you something, if you have a minute."

I nodded. I had plenty of minutes—as long as it took for the sheriff to show up and arrest me for taking Bobby's car, as a matter of fact. Plus, the tea really was good, and the chair was super comfortable, and I was so toasty warm, inside and out, that I was wondering if Mrs. Shufflebottom had a spare throw or a blanket. There's nothing better for emotional turmoil than a good six-to-eight-hour nap.

When Mrs. Shufflebottom came back, though, she was holding a book. It was a hardcover still in its dust jacket. The dust jacket was old and faded and, in spite of Mrs. Shufflebottom's best efforts, showing the faintest hints of wear. Unlike the books in the library's collection, though, this one didn't have a barcode or a spine label or the protective cover to keep the dust jacket from getting torn to ribbons. It took me a moment to realize that this book must have come from Mrs. Shufflebottom's private collection—or maybe from an archive, if the public library had such a thing.

Then I saw the title.

Death at Maplewood Manor had been Vivienne Carver's first novel—published before she helped solve the Nightingale murders and became an overnight celebrity. Of course, now I knew the truth: Vivienne hadn't helped solve the murders. *Death at Maplewood Manor* had been something of a flop, and Vivienne had needed a way back into the Forbidden City of publishing. So, she'd done what anybody would do. She'd fabricated a serial killer and framed an innocent woman, and in the process, she'd laid the foundation for a career as the self-proclaimed Matron of Murder.

It was hard to separate the truth from the memories that surged up. *Death at Maplewood Manor* had been the first Vivienne Carver book I'd read, and I'd read this same edition—part of my parents' personal library of mystery novels. The same dust jacket. The same murky art that made me grateful book cover designers had found a new direction after the 1980s. Even the smell of the yellowing paper and old glue brought me back to the first time I'd opened one of Vivienne's books. And I'd fallen in love, like most of the world, with the work of one of the best writers of our time.

When I opened the cover, I was surprised to recognize Vivienne's familiar handwriting. The inscription read, *To Agatha (that's my favorite name!), very truly yours, Vivienne Carver.*

"I wanted to show you because I know what she's done," Mrs. Shufflebottom said, "but she was a kind person, once."

I nodded, and I thought of the photo Jane had shown me of four teenagers with their whole lives ahead of them: the bright smiles, the hopeful eyes, the sense of the bond between them so palpable that it could only be called love. "I'm sure she was."

We were both silent then. From the children's section came a little boy's laughter and the murmur of a woman's voice. A middle-aged man in a baggy, collarless shirt lugged a stack of books toward the circulation desk.

Mrs. Shufflebottom cleared her throat and tapped the cover of *Death at Maplewood Manor*. In the voice of someone trying to act casual after a moment of strong emotion, she said, "It hasn't aged as well as her others, of course, but it's still a treasure." I caught a hint of a smile as she added, "Please don't let Keme startle you."

Did Mrs. Shufflebottom just make another joke? I wasn't prepared to consider that possibility.

I drank the rest of my tea (careful to keep it away from the book, of course), and tried to understand what Mrs. Shufflebottom had meant. *Death at Maplewood Manor* hadn't been an initial commercial success, but after Vivienne's star began to rise, critics—and readers—found a great deal to love in the book. I scanned the back copy, and it started to come together for me. Mrs. Shufflebottom was right; *Death at Maplewood Manor* had *not* aged as well as some of Vivienne's other work, mostly because the book was built around a shocking revelation that, in 2018, was significantly less shocking.

The twist had to do with the victim's affair. Throughout the book, it was clear that figuring out the identity of the victim's romantic partner—the last person to see her alive at a midnight tryst—was the key to the whole mystery.

And Vivienne *did* manage to shock people—in 1987. Because in *Death at Maplewood Manor*, the twist was that the victim's lover was *a woman!!!!!!!* (Shock. Awe. Gasps.) (God, using that many exclamation marks felt unbelievably liberating.) So, in that sense, Mrs. Shufflebottom was right—the novel felt dated. Homosexual relationships didn't (or shouldn't) have shock value anymore, and trying to use them that way went against decades of work to normalize them.

On the other hand, like most of Vivienne's work, it was a master class in the craft of mystery. One of the reasons the twist worked so well in *Death at Maplewood Manor* is that Vivienne never does anything so crass as have a character say, "Well, she was a red-blooded American woman, so we're looking for a man." Instead, she let the reader's assumptions do the work for her; most readers, like the other characters in the book, simply *assume* that the victim's lover would be a man. It was an excellent example of an old saw among mystery writers: *readers will mislead themselves.* All you have to do is show them what's happening, and they'll make up their own story—and, bonus, it'll be much more convincing than any red herrings or misdirection you could fabricate on your own.

All the great mystery authors do it to greater or lesser extents. Elizabeth George does it in her Inspector Lynley novels—while investigating a suspect's home, Lynley finds a shrine to his wife. The implication—and the reader's assumption—is that the woman is dead, and the shrine is a display of grief. But it turns out (spoiler alert!) *she's alive!!!!!!!* (I'm serious, it feels amazing. You should try it sometime.) Daphne du Maurier does it—that's basically (spoiler alert) the entire plot of *Rebecca!!!!!!!* (Okay, that one felt like too much.) Agatha Christie was so good she could do it over and over again, and somehow she always made it work. And, of course, Vivienne had done it here, as well as in many other novels.

Holding *Death at Maplewood Manor* in my hands, I couldn't help but wonder how much of the plot, with that final revelation of an illicit lesbian relationship, had been born out of Vivienne's life. It's a fallacy, and a dangerous one, to conflate an author with their characters, but it was Vivienne's first book, and she'd written it so close to the events that had devastated her emotionally—the death of her brother, the loss of her lover, the decision to leave behind everything and stake her future on the belief that she was capable of greatness. Was it really so much of a stretch to think that the immediacy and power of that time in her life must have shaped the story she was telling?

It would be nice if it did, I thought with wry weariness. It would be lovely if I could flip through the book, spot an easy analogue for Richard's death, and identify the killer all these years later. As though it were a secret Vivienne had buried in the text for someone else to find. Of course, that was nonsense—if she'd known who had killed Richard, she never would have hired me in the first place. Still, it was a fun idea. I tried to think of a mystery novel that featured a sleuth who solved a crime in the past by unraveling the plot of a novel. The Josephine Tey book came closest. It wouldn't even be all that difficult to work in that trick about having the reader mislead themselves. I mean, it happened in real life all the time—look at me. I'd assumed Vivienne and Jane had been straight simply because they'd married men—

The revelation had a physical weight, dropping in my gut. Richard's distance from his father. Richard's arguments with everyone in his final months. Neil and Jane. Neil wearing Richard's bracelet.

I was an idiot, I decided.

I laid Mrs. Shufflebottom's book on the counter, shouted, "Thanks for the tea!" and sprinted for the door.

Mrs. Shufflebottom's polite—but stern—"Inside voice, Dashiell," floated after me into the night.

CHAPTER 16

The drive to Astoria (in Bobby's SUV) was a blur of darkness, wind-stirred trees, and the oil-paint texture of the ag fields. I tried to keep my attention on the road, but my mind was racing, turning over everything, trying to make the pieces fit. Twice, I caught myself doing 90 on roads that were like black ice, slick with the night mist that gathered along the coast, and I had to force myself to ease off the gas.

I was still in a state somewhere between excitement and stupefaction when I turned onto that familiar street outside Astoria. In a few of the little white bungalows, light showed in the windows, but Arlen's house was dark, and so was Neil and Jane's. I parked, reached for the door, and stopped as a second realization hit me—this one like cold water.

I had driven out here in a frenzy, determined to confront this family and learn the truth. But in my excitement, I'd overlooked one important detail: someone had tried to kill me. Someone didn't want the truth about Richard's death coming to light. Someone was willing to do whatever it took to stop me. And that person was here, I was sure—one of the people I was about to face.

My hesitation only lasted a moment. I was exhausted—physically and emotionally. I was exhilarated by that feeling of the pieces of a puzzle falling together. And the aftermath of my fight with Bobby was evolving from grief into a low-grade fever and the need to sink my teeth into somebody.

I dropped out of the SUV and jogged across the street.

When I knocked on Neil and Jane's door, only silence answered. I counted to thirty and tried again. I'd lost track of the time, so I checked my phone. At some point, I'd missed a call from Indira, and the group text had blown up. I ignored all of that. It was 9:30. I knocked again.

This time, on the other side of the door, footsteps came toward me, and then Neil asked, "Who is it?"

"Dash Dane. I need to talk to you and Jane."

The deadbolt thunked back. The door opened. Neil was dressed in blue-striped pajamas, and his hair was sticking up in back; out of uniform, he looked older. Behind him, Jane was cinching the belt on her robe.

"I need to talk to you right now," I said. "About Richard. I know what happened."

Something changed on Neil's face. Just a flicker, but I was sure I'd seen it. He didn't look back at Jane, but I could tell he was fighting the urge. Then, with forced heartiness, he said, "Well, I don't know about that. But if you've got something to say, I guess we'd better hear it."

He put his hand in the pocket of his pajamas as he stepped back.

This was my chance to turn back, I knew. I could run to the Pilot. Call Bobby. Do the sensible thing.

But what I *wanted* to do was bite the sensible thing right in the heinie. So, I stepped inside.

Jane was turning on lamps, and the little click of each switch was the only sound. The lamps left deep shadows, and the house smelled like something floral, and there were fresh vacuum lines in the carpet. Neil motioned me to the sofa, and I sat. Jane took an armchair. Neil stood behind her, one hand still in his pocket.

"Is it true you and Vivienne were lovers?" I asked.

It wasn't surprise that flashed across Jane's face. It was pain. The realization left me off-balance; after all these years, the fact that it could still hurt her so much.

All she said was "Yes."

I took a deep breath and dried my palms on my jeans. I looked at Neil. "I wondered why the four of you were so close. It's not uncommon; I know that. A tight group of friends, especially in high school. Even, in a small town, for a group of friends like that to remain tight after they graduate. But the more I learned, the more I started to wonder. You were *so* close. Even after the divorce, when by all rights, the relationships should have soured. Even after Richard's death. And there was all that business about Vivienne's relationship with Neil, how quickly they realized it wasn't going to work out, that kind of thing. Your comment, Neil, about how Candy was oblivious to the fact that she didn't have a chance with you. And then I realized what it all meant. You—"

"I'm gay," Neil said quietly. "Richard was my boyfriend." His dark eyes were lost in shadow, and he gave a strange half-laugh. "He would have *hated* me using that word."

"Okay, here's the deal. I was right about to do my thing where I reveal—" I blew out a breath. "Doesn't matter. The point is, all the fighting, those nasty fights between you and Richard, were because—"

"I wanted him to come out. With me."

"Seriously? Could you just let me have, like, one thing?"

"I was insistent. In high school, it had been easy enough to—to pretend to be something else. People were happy to see what was on the surface, and we were all still figuring everything out."

"It was Vivienne's plan," Jane said softly. "She was always the smartest of us. We'd keep doing what we'd been doing. We'd get married. We'd be friends. We'd live our lives without anyone having to know."

"She was always smart," Neil agreed. "But she was a child. We all were. She didn't understand what it would be like to live a lie forever. She didn't know what it would feel like to be in love, and to never be able to let anyone know."

"Richard—" I began.

"Didn't want to come out, of course," Jane said.

"You too?" I asked. "Try this: just wait until I finish a sentence."

"I think that's why Vivienne came up with the plan in the first place. She loved Richard. She thought she was helping him."

"He was terrified of coming out," Neil said. "Terrified of his father's reaction. Terrified of what the town would say. Terrified—" His mouth twisted, and he put his hand on Jane's shoulder. "Terrified I would ask too much."

"Like Vivienne," I said.

Jane nodded.

When Neil spoke again, his voice grew tight with frustration. "He was too afraid to take a chance. He thought everything could stay the same, that we could go on the way we always had."

"But things never stay the same," I said. "Do they?"

"No, they don't. I certainly didn't. Richard didn't, no matter how much he tried to convince himself otherwise. After Vivienne and I had tried to—tried to make a go of it, I knew we couldn't keep it up. But the more I tried to push Richard, the worse it got."

"You loved him," Jane said. "You're being too hard on yourself."

Neil shook his head. It was hard to tell, with most of his face lost in shadow, but I thought he was crying. His voice was clear enough, though, when he spoke. "I didn't understand, then, that there are some people who will choose being safe even if it means being unhappy. They might even manage to believe everything's okay, so long as they don't have to face the truth."

The floral smell was gone now, and in its place, creeping through the dark of the house, came the stagnant smell of the slough.

"But you two—" I began.

"We decided to live together," Jane said.

(I couldn't even be mad about the interruption.)

"After a few years," she continued, "when it was obvious neither one of us was going to…to move on, I suppose, it seemed the obvious thing to do."

"I don't understand," I said. "Why?" Jane met my question with a blank expression. When I turned to Neil, I thought I heard him draw in a breath. "You were going to come out. I thought you were done hiding. Why didn't you—" I almost said *find someone else*, but I heard how callous it sounded, and I managed to stop myself.

Neil must have heard the words anyway, though, because he said, as though stating a simple fact, "Richard was gone. There wasn't anyone else."

In the distance, an engine rumbled through the night.

Jane reached over her shoulder to pat Neil's hand, but her eyes stayed on me. "There you go, Mr. Dane. Did you ask what you wanted to ask?"

I nodded, but I said, "Richard wasn't murdered, was he? Richard—"

"Say one more word—" a crusty voice said, and then a footfall came from the hall, and Arlen stepped into the room. He leveled the old shotgun at me. "—and I'll blow your head off."

CHAPTER 17

I sat there, staring down the barrels of Arlen's ancient shotgun. Arlen himself looked like something dragged out of the grave: his stringy white hair in a frenzy, his face gaunt and pale, a tic working restlessly in his eye. The smell of the slough was so thick it was almost suffocating, but under it, I caught a hint of body odor and liniment.

"What's wrong with you?" Arlen asked. The shotgun trembled in his hands. "Why can't you leave decent people alone? You had to come snooping around, stirring things up. Why couldn't you take a hint?"

"Arlen," Neil said, "put that down."

"Don't move," Arlen barked at him. "I know about you. I know about all of you. You think you could keep it a secret, hide it, make a fool out of me. Laughing at me all these years."

"No one was laughing at you, Arlen," Jane said.

"He was my son! He was gone!" And then Arlen's voice quavered, and he sounded his age. "Wasn't that enough?"

"He wasn't gone," I said. My brain was racing, trying to put together the final piece of the puzzle. Someone had wanted to stop me. Someone had wanted the truth of Richard's death to remain a secret. And now I knew it had been Arlen who had run me off the road. Arlen who had wanted to bury the past. But why? I tried to remember what I knew about this man. He'd been furious about Candy's relationships with men, including Zane. He'd been head of the Astoria lodge of the Sons of Sweden. He'd fought incessantly with Richard. "Richard wasn't gone," I said again. "He—"

But Arlen braced the shotgun against his shoulder, steadying his aim, and I cut off.

"He didn't run away, Arlen," Jane said.

Neil breathed out hard and said, "He killed himself."

A spasm of pain contorted Arlen's body. Pure, raw grief—undiluted by the passage of the years. A distant part of me wondered if, twisted by the physical agony of the loss, Arlen might pull the trigger without even realizing it. But another part of me realized that whatever happened, it was beyond my control.

"No," Arlen managed to say. "No. Not my son. Not my son. No, he wouldn't. I saw him—"

And then I knew.

Jane and Richard had fought.

Jane had left.

Vivienne and Candy had both been gone.

And Arlen had been home, tending to his sick wife.

"Richard told you," I said. My voice sounded scratchy even to me. "After the fight with Jane. He walked next door and told you—"

"What?" Neil asked.

Arlen shouted, "No!"

"He told you?" Neil was shouting too now. He sounded almost hysterical, the words shrill and uneven. "What did you say? What did you *do*?"

"He didn't tell me anything!" The scream was so raw that Arlen's words were barely intelligible. "He came over to pick a fight, the way he always did. That's all he ever wanted—to make me angry, to make a fool out of me, to make me a joke in the eyes of every decent man in this town. The things he was saying—" Arlen gulped air, and I thought he was no longer here. He was somewhere else, sometime long ago. "I told him to knock it off. I told him this wasn't a joke. And he said no, it wasn't a joke. He said—" Arlen's voice broke. "He said he was sorry."

Our breaths were ragged, unkempt things, rising and falling in the dark.

When Arlen spoke again, his voice was dull. "I told him he was no son of mine. I told him I never wanted to see him again. I'd kill him if I ever saw him again." He couldn't seem to stand up straight anymore, and his labored breathing was like a heartbeat. The muzzle of the shotgun slipped away from me. "That's why he ran away."

Jane was crying softly, her head in her hands.

"He didn't run away!" Neil shouted. "He killed himself, you stupid old man. He was right here, the bottle of pills on the floor next to him. We had to take care of him! *We* did! *We* loved him, *we* were his family, and he did that to us! Because of you! He was everything to me, and you took him away from me!"

Arlen shook his head, his expression empty, not hearing—or not wanting to hear—any of us.

I looked at Jane.

The color had drained from her face. She touched her forehead and squeezed her eyes shut, but after a moment, she began to speak. "I came home that night." She stopped, and in the caesura that followed was the whole tragedy. Then, somehow, she started again. "I didn't know what to do. Vivienne was God only knew where—gone to help Candy, I found out later. I didn't want Neil to see Richard like that, but I didn't know what else to do."

"No," Neil said. An ugly flush filled his face, and his chest rose and fell with a limping unevenness. "No. He was mine. I needed to be there." I thought that might have been all, but then he said, "He would have wanted it that way, Jane. He would have wanted to do right by you. Just like he would have wanted Viv to have enough money to move, so we gave it to her. Just like he would have wanted us to take care of each other."

Maybe the question was on my face because when Jane opened her eyes, she looked at me and said, "The life insurance. Neil said—"

"He would have wanted it that way," Neil said again. "He was sick. He didn't know what he was doing."

Jane shook her head, wiping her eyes. "It seems like a dream now. Like someone else did it. I don't know what we were thinking. I don't know why it seemed like the right thing to do."

"You did this," Arlen said, and for a disorienting moment, I thought he was talking to me. But he raised his head, and voice muzzy, spoke to Neil. "You did it to him. You made him that way. No son of mine—"

Arlen swept the barrel of the gun toward Neil.

With a wordless shout, Neil lunged at the old man.

The front door crashed open.

Bobby stood there, scanning the room. He was still in the tank and shorts, but he was carrying his service weapon. Maybe it was the weak lighting of the living room, or maybe it was some strong emotion that seemed to grip him—whatever the reason, in that first moment I saw him, I almost didn't recognize him.

"Sheriff's deputy," he shouted. "Drop the—"

Arlen swung the gun at Bobby.

At the same moment, I pushed off from the sofa and flew across the room. I crashed into Arlen. He grunted as we tumbled into the wall. The shotgun whacked me on the shoulder. Then the gun went off, and the sound of the shot rang in my ears.

We hit the floor and separated, and I rolled across the carpet. I scrambled to my feet, looking for Arlen and the gun.

Neil stood over him; he'd wrested the shotgun away from Arlen, and he cried as he held it. Arlen lay on his back, eyes wide and staring, so still that I thought maybe he was dead.

When I looked over, a hole in the plaster showed me where the shot had gone. It was inches from Bobby's head. Darkness rushed up at me, and I thought I might pass out.

But I didn't. I heard Bobby taking the gun from Neil. And then Bobby was by me, his arm around my waist, holding me up—or maybe just holding me—as sirens came out of the night.

Chapter 18

The Astoria police wanted to interview me, of course, after they separated all of us. I tried to answer their questions as best I could, but it was hard to focus on what they were saying, much less on how I was responding. My thoughts kept going back to the feeling of the shotgun bucking against my arm, the clap of gunfire, the panic when I hadn't known what had happened. If Bobby had been hurt. I remembered seeing where the shot had gone into the wall, inches from his head. I had to close my eyes, and one of the detectives got me a paper bag to breathe into, which weirdly enough actually helped. It was easier to think about Bobby commandeering Fox's van to come after me.

I did, eventually, manage to get the gist of their questions. They weren't exactly thrilled that I'd been operating solo (big surprise), but that was small change compared to how angry they were that I'd helped exonerate Vivienne. A suicide wasn't national news—not even a suicide that had been covered up for thirty years. To say the detectives were disappointed would be putting it mildly.

Eventually, Sheriff Acosta showed up (presumably, because they had to get her permission before they put me in front of the firing squad). She talked to the Astoria officer who seemed to be in charge, and after what looked like a *lot* of arguing, she came over and retrieved me.

"You're going to have to come back tomorrow and make an official statement," Acosta said. She looked tired. "I recommend bringing your attorney."

"I'm sorry," I said.

She nodded. "Let me get Bobby, and I'll follow you home."

"Is he okay?" I hadn't seen him since the police had sent us to sit in separate squad cars. "Is he in trouble?"

Acosta gave me a funny look.

But before she could answer, one of the Astoria detectives shouted, "What do you mean she's taking them?"

"You go get him," Acosta said to me. "I'll handle this."

"Where—"

"Back of the ambulance."

I started to ask what happened, but then I realized it didn't matter.

Let me tell you something: if you want to see a little gay boy *run*.

I don't even remember crossing the distance—it was a blur of flashing lights and the darkness that swept in on their wake. But I remember when I saw him sitting on the tailgate, a blanket around his shoulders, in the steady light from the back of the ambulance. He had his head in his hands, his elbows on his knees, and he was sitting so very still.

Somehow, I managed to hit the brakes and not barrel into him and hug him, Millie style, into a million pieces. I slowed to a walk. I took the last few steps so slowly, in fact, that it felt like it took me years to finally reach him. He must have heard me because he looked up. His face was drawn with something beyond exhaustion. The earthy bronze of his eyes was dim. Even his regulation hair looked wild, like someone had been running their hands through it.

All of a sudden, I realized I was going to have to say something, and the last words we'd said to each other had been so awful. So angry.

But I am, forever and always, Dashiell Dawson Dane, which means I did the *weirdest* little wave and heard myself say, "Hi."

It felt like a long time before Bobby said, "Hi."

There was probably a stoic, masculine way to approach the next part of this interaction—something that would allow both of us to feel appropriately butch, without either of us making ourselves vulnerable or sacrificing our pride.

Which was why it made perfect sense that, instead, I blurted, "Are you okay?"

Another long pause came. Bobby shook his head.

The seconds ticked past. A paramedic came around the back of the ambulance, typing a message on her phone. When she saw us, she took one look, rolled her eyes, and went back the way she'd come.

I decided that was a sign that the universe wasn't going to put a merciful end to this conversation for me. So, I climbed up onto the tailgate next to Bobby. I mean, not right next to him. Because, you know, the fight. And because he probably wanted his space. And also just in case either of us needed to make a quick escape.

"Please don't die."

The words escaped me before I could stop them.

(Yep, still good old Dash.)

Bobby craned his head to look at me. "What?"

"Don't die. Please don't die."

"I'm not going to die. He didn't shoot me." That unreadable emotion tightened his expression again, and he said, voice stiff, "I had another panic attack."

"No, I mean don't ever die. Please, Bobby. Please don't ever die from anything. Because it would kill me. You can't ever let anything bad happen to you. No more guns. No more surfing. Definitely no more working out. I mean, my God, Bobby, the human body isn't meant to lift all that heavy stuff." I managed to come to a crashing halt. And then I forced myself to say, "He almost shot you."

And in my mind, I heard Neil say, *Richard was gone. There wasn't anyone else.*

Bobby didn't say anything, but his breathing sounded accelerated. And then it sounded even worse. And I realized, a moment later (because I'm so smart) what was happening.

"No," I said. "No, no." I rubbed his back through the blanket. "Everything's okay. Deep breaths. Deep, slow breaths."

Through punched-out gasps, Bobby said, "I saw the gun. I got there. Saw that gun. And he was. He was pointing it. Right at you. And—"

He stopped to suck in air.

I shushed him. "It's okay. We were both scared."

But Bobby shook his head. "Not okay. Want to. Tell you. Need to—"

He had to stop again to suck in air.

"How about I tell you something?" I asked. "How about I tell you something instead, and then, later, when you're feeling better, you can tell me?"

He didn't answer. He was taking those thin, horrible breaths. But he didn't try to speak again, so I took that as a yes.

As I rubbed his back some more, I thought about what to say. The cleverest way. The most poetic way. The most powerful, heartfelt way.

But, since I'd already been doing such a great job tonight, all that came out was "I love you."

Bobby seemed to get smaller, shoulders shrinking, pressing his head into his hands.

"I'm sorry," I said. "No, actually, you know what? I'm not sorry. Well, I'm sorry it took me so long, I guess, but I'm not sorry for telling you." I waited for the waves of throat-clenching panic, the lightheadedness, the vertigo. But instead, I felt…not calm, but shocked into something else. Detached, maybe, like the night's events had left me partially dissociated, and I was watching myself in slow motion as I staged the single most impressive self-destruction sequence in history. "I'm sorry if you didn't want to hear that, or if it makes your life complicated, or if it's going to make you have another panic attack, Bobby. I am. But I had to tell you. Tonight, there was this moment where I thought you might be dead—" And now it did come—not my anxiety, not my constant indecisiveness, but terror. It was a physical sensation, sharp and unyielding, like a knife being forced into my chest. "Bobby, I thought you were *dead.*"

He didn't move. The blanket whispered softly against his clothes; he was trembling, I realized, and his breathing was ragged and high.

"All I could think," I said, "all I've been able to think ever since I saw how close that shot came to you, is what if? What if I'd lost you? What if I never got to see you again, or talk to you until you told me you really had to go to work now, or explain the entire plot of a nine-book mystery series I'm never going to write?" I had to swallow. The numbness still gave me some sense of distance from myself, and I was starting to wonder if my judgment was impaired—if tomorrow, when I was the same old neurotic Dash again, I would realize I'd made a terrible mistake. But I kept going. I had to keep going. "I've been thinking about that a lot the last few days. Because of Vivienne and Jane. And Richard and Neil. God, you don't even know—I'll have to tell you all about it. The point is, I look at them, and I look at what they never got to have. Jane never got what she wanted because Vivienne was selfish, because she was worried about her career and her reputation, but most of all, because she was afraid. Afraid to take a risk. And Richard was the same way, right up until the end. Neil said after Richard was gone, there wasn't anybody else, and I've been thinking about that too. If you were gone. If I lost you."

Emergency lights bobbed and spun. Bobby didn't look at me. He still didn't say anything.

"So, I've been thinking, what if I never got to tell you that you're strong, and you're sweet, and maybe most importantly, you're kind? What if I never got to tell you all the reasons I love you? I love that you're patient with me. I love your big, goofy smile. I love that you care if I'm warm enough or if I'm comfortable or if I've had enough coffee for one day. I love that you're my friend,

Bobby, because you *are* my friend. You're the first person I think about, you know that? With everything. When I see something on *Crime Cats*, I want to text it to you. When I'm going to bed, I remember some dumb thing I did that almost made you smile. When I'm reading in the billiard room now, I look over and expect to see you lying on the floor, ear buds in, listening to your music. When Indira makes a really good cake."

His hands moved restlessly over his face. I could hear his breath whistling in his throat. The smell of the asphalt, releasing its lingering warmth from the day, wafted up to us.

Rubbing his back, I said, "I promise I'm almost done, and I'll leave you alone. I just—I just needed you to know. I came here because I wasn't in love with Hugo, but also because I needed to figure myself out. I wasn't even sure love was real, and if it was, I didn't know if I'd ever recognize it when I felt it. I'm such a mess, Bobby. I can't decide who my fictional detective is going to be. I freak out about social situations with even the tiniest bit of ambiguity. For heaven's sake, you've seen how long it takes me just to pick a flavor of ice cream." I took a breath. "Lawrence Block has one of his characters say, 'Whatever love means, it's how I feel about you,' and that's it. That's exactly it. This is love, what I feel for you. It's like there isn't room inside me for anything else. This is it, and it's real, and it's everything I wanted, and I love you so much that I can't— I can't even put it into words, really. And it makes me so happy that it's you. So, I wanted to thank you for giving me this, because it couldn't have been anybody else. And I wanted to tell you how much you mean to me. I don't want to die without telling you. And I know this is crazy, and maybe it feels like it's coming out of left field because we've never gone on a date or kissed or done anything the way people say you're supposed to do it. But none of that matters. What matters is I love you. I love you, Bobby."

A shiver worked its way down Bobby's broad back. He sat up so suddenly that I thought maybe the panic attack had finally arrived in full. When he turned to face me, his eyes were wet, and he was gulping air. And this, that detached part of me knew, was Bobby: to the very last, still fighting for control.

"It's okay," I said, and I was surprised to find myself smiling. "You don't have to say anything. I know it's—it's hard for you to talk about this kind of stuff, and Keme's right: not everyone has to put their feelings into words the way I do. There are so many ways you let me know I'm your friend and you care about me, so many things you do for me, without ever saying anything. So, I'm not asking you to say anything or do anything or change anything. I just wanted you to know how I feel. If you don't feel the same way, that's okay. If you never want to talk about this again, that's okay too. If we're just going to be friends forever, it would still be the best thing that ever happened to me. But please don't die, Bobby—like, ever. For one thing, there wouldn't be anyone to defend me, and Keme would definitely make me do pull-ups. And I immediately regret making a joke, but I think I am, uh, suddenly super nervous."

And I was. At that exact moment, it all caught up to me: everything I'd said, all the rambling, disjointed, adolescent sentiments that sounded like they'd been copyedited out of an issue of *Teen Vogue*. That sense of detachment popped like a bubble, and heat rushed into my face. My head suddenly felt like it was filled with bees.

And Bobby was still staring at me. The rich, earthy gold of his eyes shone like glass behind the sheen of tears. His pupils were huge. His lips were parted, and his chest fell and rose in painful-looking hitches. And I knew, without anyone having to tell me. What had happened. He wasn't going to say anything. He couldn't, even if he wanted to. The distress in his expression told me that whether Bobby felt the same way I did, or he simply wanted to tell me to screw off, he just couldn't do it. He had told me once, what seemed like a long time ago, that when he tried to talk about the things that mattered most to him, terror made it feel like knives were spinning in his gut. And even through my embarrassment, my heart hurt for him, because he was Bobby, and I did love him.

"I'll leave you alone," I said, sliding to the edge of the tailgate. "Do you want me to get the paramedic—"

He lunged toward me, the movement jerky and broken, without any of his usual grace. His hands caught my head: fingers curling along my neck, palms settled at my jawline, thumbs brushing my cheekbones. He had calluses from all that surfing, and the slight roughness of his hands startled a breath out of me. I caught a whiff of that clean, sporty scent that at this point I was *sure* had to be his deodorant, and then he pulled me to him and kissed me.

I won't go on and on about it. I mean, a gentleman doesn't kiss and tell.

But if you've ever been kissed, really kissed, by someone you want in all the ways it's possible to want someone, then you know.

(Okay, I'll say *this*: toe-curling doesn't even begin to describe it.)

When he released me, he looked punch drunk, barely able to keep himself upright as he took deep, uneven breaths. But to be fair, I probably looked pretty much the same.

And then that big, beautiful, goofy smile slipped out. A little uncertain, maybe. But real.

My grin was so big it hurt my cheeks. And because I am perpetually, inescapably, Dashiell Dawson Dane, I heard myself say, "See? Talking is overrated."

Chapter 19

When we got home, it was the small hours of the morning. We walked through the house in the dark. Our steps whispered on the heirloom rugs. I paused at the top of the landing—to say good night, I guess. (Okay, I was hoping for a goodnight kiss at the *minimum*.) Bobby surprised me by putting a hand at the small of my back and guiding me into my room. He shut the door behind him, and then his hand found the small of my back again, and he walked me to the bed.

I opened my mouth.

"No monkey business," he said before I had a chance to ask what was happening. His voice almost sounded back to normal, and there was even a hint of playfulness. Then he hesitated and said, "I want to be near you tonight. Please?"

Well, how was I supposed to say no to that?

By the light of a single lamp, we changed into sleep shorts and tees. It was different, now, getting to appreciate those glimpses of Bobby without a shirt—the defined chest, the strong arms, the wide shoulders. And, of course, it's hard not to appreciate a gentleman who knows how to fill out a white tee and a pair of mesh shorts.

"Unh-uh," he said when he caught me looking. He nudged me toward the canopy bed. "I told you: no funny stuff."

"We're adults."

He made a *mmm* noise that suggested this was up for debate.

"Nobody would know," I tried.

Bobby gave me a look that reminded me—pointedly—of the Deputy Bobby I had first met.

"It gets pretty hot in here sometimes," I said. "You should probably take that shirt off."

He put his hand over my mouth, which was good because I couldn't stop laughing. When I did, though, he peeled his fingers away, kissed me, and looked at me for what felt like a long time, his expression earnest and searching and serious, before he finally said, "Goodnight."

"Goodnight," I whispered.

It had been a long time since someone had touched me. And—not trying to take a dig at the previous men in my life—it was so *different* with Bobby. There were so many other emotions, deeper emotions, layered into the experience. Which is one way of explaining that even though I was exhausted, I was sure I'd never sleep. My, er, situation didn't improve when Bobby rolled onto his side, pulled me against him, and proved, immediately and without any trace of doubt, that he was the single best big spoon in the history of the world. His breath felt good on my neck. I liked the faint rasp of a day's worth of stubble when he repositioned his head. His arm was solid, draped over me. My tee had ridden up, and his thumb scratched pleasantly at my bare stomach.

Look, I was *never* going to get to sleep.

"It's not that I don't want to," Bobby said.

"Oh good," I said, "because I *definitely* want to." His slight pause made me realize I'd misread the meaning of his sentence. "Uh, I mean, go on."

"I want to…talk." He took a deep breath. "To tell you." His silence lasted longer this time, broken by those deep breaths that made me think of the movement of the sea. "God, why is this so hard?"

I rubbed his arm. "There's been a lot going on the last few days. Talking about that kind of stuff is already scary and hard because we're making ourselves vulnerable."

"It didn't seem hard for you."

"I was in a weird headspace. And things have been extra stressful the last few days—Arlen did try to kill me twice, so they've definitely been stressful for me."

"When I saw the Jeep at the bottom of that hill, I thought—" His voice frayed until he couldn't go on. When he spoke again, the words were wire thin. "I wanted to tell you. Right then. I thought about what could have happened to you, and I knew I needed to tell you. And as soon as I opened my mouth—"

A second passed. And then another. I said, "Panic attack?"

He nodded into my shoulder.

I made shushing sounds and rubbed his arm some more.

"And then tonight, you were being so brave." His voice still had that brittle tension. "I wanted to tell you how proud I was of you, because I knew how hard that was for you. I wanted to tell you—" But he stopped again. He was vibrating against me, in the throes of those warring emotions.

I shushed him again and said, "I know, Bobby. You don't have to tell me. You definitely better not tell me tonight, or that prohibition on monkey business is going right out the window."

His laugh was wet and unsteady.

I brought his hand to my mouth and kissed his knuckles. "You'll feel better in the morning."

He didn't say anything to that, but he kissed the back of my neck, and *let me tell you*, after that, it was official. I wasn't going to get any sleep. Probably ever. I was going to die like this.

(The word *unsatisfied* comes to mind.)

And then, of course, I pretty much immediately passed out.

When I woke up, Bobby was gone, which made me suspect he might be part ninja. The quality of the light filtering in around the curtains made me think it was still early, and the sound of the waves was steady. I lay there awhile. I mean, the house wasn't on fire, and there was no reason to jump out of bed. Especially if the alternative was to stay snuggled up in bed, remembering how a certain deputy-slash-ninja felt when he was pressed up against you. (Did you know if a guy has muscles, like, *real* muscles, he is surprisingly *not* squishy. I mean, not that I mind.)

I was still in that state where my brain hadn't fully woken up yet, and my thoughts had a lucidity that was relaxed and somehow not quite logical, when Hugo popped into my head. (Let me tell you: if your ex flashing through your brain doesn't put any and all romantical thoughts on ice, nothing will.) Even worse was when I remembered I was supposed to write with him today. I was *supposed* to have finished my scene of *The Next Night*. That ugly, cowardly little episode when Dexter Drake hid in the bushes and waited for the police to finish arresting his lover. As he had before, of course, so many times. And as he would again. Because for Dexter Drake, the next night would be the same as all the ones that had come before: dark, long, and lonely.

(That was pretty good, and I was definitely going to tell Hugo.)

But I also needed to tell him that I didn't like the story we were writing. Maybe it was too late to change it. Maybe not. But I needed to tell him because, once again, I hadn't been honest with him, and I was starting to suspect that there was more of Dexter Drake in me (or was it the other way around?) than I wanted to admit.

The problem, of course, was that Hugo knew what he was doing. Hugo had an artistic vision. Hugo was a published author. A successful author. And he was doing me a favor—a huge one, actually—by bringing me on as his co-author. What was I going to suggest instead of the story we'd been working on? One of the million different versions of Will Gower? Will Gower the lion tamer? (He solved mysteries with a traveling circus in the 1930s.) Will Gower the professional water slide tester? (Hear me out: *lots* of people die at water parks.) Will Gower the spy on the run? (He *definitely* didn't have a squishy body.)

And it wasn't only the fact that I couldn't decide on a version of Will Gower—although, in my defense, I'd been making progress, and I had an actual manuscript with an actual story. Kind of. The bigger issue was that the more I experienced the world, the more I found myself (against my better judgment, trust me) caught up in real-life mysteries and crimes and murders, the more I realized that the mysteries I'd been writing were too…small. Maybe that wasn't exactly the word (I mean, it's not like words were my job or anything), but it came close. The mysteries I'd been writing seemed so limited in scope, in complexity, in humanity. No matter how convoluted the puzzle, no matter how richly drawn the characters, in the end, the story only lived for ninety thousand words or so. In real life, tragedy didn't end. It just kept unspooling across lives. And generations.

And what about stories like Richard's and Jane's and Neil's and, yes, Vivienne's? And even Arlen's and Candy's? The promise of a crime novel was that the truth would be uncovered and justice would be served. But was that justice, what I'd done for Richard? Vivienne would know the truth, and that was something. But that same truth had broken an old man's heart, shattered his vision of himself and his son. Maybe Arlen got what he deserved, but if that was justice, it tasted like ashes. I thought of the strange conversation I'd had with Jane when I'd first visited her. How brash I'd been, insisting that the justice I offered was worth any price, and the way her silence had swallowed my words. I should have suspected, then. But, of course, I hadn't.

The thought, though, made something stir at the back of my head. A hint of an idea. I tried to chase it down. Maybe I'd been spending too much time with Bobby, because an earnest, serious voice inside my head told me that I was thinking about it all wrong. Yes, one aspect of justice was that wrongdoers were punished. And that was an important part of it. But justice was more than that.

Had to be more than that. Because punishment didn't undo the wrong that was done. Punishment couldn't bring back a dead son, a dead lover, a dead brother. Sometimes, there was no one to punish. Because, in other words, in the end, punishment didn't change anything.

But there *was* another aspect to justice. More to it, I guess, although maybe even that wasn't the right way to say it. Justice wasn't only about punishing people who broke the law. Justice was…a promise. Maybe the fundamental promise, the one we made each other when humans first agreed to share their fire as a shield against the night. The promise to care for each other. To protect each other. The promise that if evil came for you, you would not be alone.

And in that half-waking lucidity, my brain drew a line from justice to stories. Because wasn't that the fundamental promise of a story, as well? For the storyteller, it was the promise that the storyteller wasn't speaking into the void—that there were other people out there, people with the same dreams and hopes and hurts, and they would hear and understand? And that promise worked the other way as well. Because the real magic of a story—as anyone who loves books can tell you—happened when you read something on the page that you thought only you had ever known and felt, and in that instant, you were connected to someone who might have lived thousands of miles away, who might have died hundreds of years ago, but who was, nevertheless, like you. That was the promise of a story. The promise of knowing and being known, mind to mind, heart to heart.

The story came to me the way my best ideas always had: a series of lightning strikes, and then everything cohering into something that felt bigger than me, electric, alive.

I bolted out of my room, down the stairs, and as I spun toward the den, I almost crashed into Indira and Fox.

"Dashiell—" Indira said, but then she caught a look at me, and her tone hardened into something serious. "What happened?" And then, in an even *unhappier* tone, she demanded, "You didn't cock it up, did you?"

"I just had—" I stopped. "What is happening with everyone's language?"

Fox was studying me with an interest bordering on the scientific. "Did you honestly use an extremely ambiguous quote from a mystery novel to tell Bobby you loved him?"

"How could you possibly know—I don't have to answer that." I drew myself up with as much dignity as I could muster, considering (I realized at that moment) I was wearing nothing more than a white tank and black trunks with a rainbow-colored Xbox controller in, um, a certain spot. "I don't have time for this. I just invented cozy noir."

"What is that?" Indira asked.

"Well, I don't know entirely. I invented it, like, two minutes ago." The idea had started to lose some of its charge, although I thought some of that might have been because I was standing around in my skivvies. "Also, I have no idea if it's even possible."

"Anything's possible if you're willing to make enough mistakes along the way," Fox said, and to my surprise, they turned me toward the den and gave me a shove. "So if anyone can do it, it's you."

"Uh, thank you?"

But they just kept pushing me into the den, and they shut the door behind me.

Since I was now a prisoner in my own house, I decided I'd better get to work. I found a hoodie that I'd forgotten in the den at some point and zipped it up. I got settled in my favorite chair with my favorite blanket. I grabbed my laptop. When I touched the track pad, though, I hesitated.

I mean, would it be the worst thing in the world if I took a quick—like, *super* quick—peek at *Crime Cats?* Ideas needed time to…percolate. And I definitely didn't want to rush into anything—

My phone buzzed with a text message from Hugo. *You up?*

All of a sudden, I knew how today was going to go. I was going to make excuses. I was going to find a way to weasel out of all the decisions I'd made in that warm, sleepy safety of my bed. I wouldn't tell Hugo about the book. The idea of Will Gower in some sort of cozy noir story would fade farther and farther away. I might not have been in exactly this position before, but I knew myself, and I could feel it happening.

A rap at the door made me burst out, "Oh thank God," in a way that sounded marginally unhinged.

Bobby stuck his head in, his expression quizzical, before coming the rest of the way into the den. "I don't want to interrupt—"

"No, God, you're not interrupting." I was scrambling to my feet before I remembered my current state of dress, and I barely caught the blanket before it fell. But then, Bobby had slept next to me in these clothes, so it wasn't exactly new to him. He, of course, looked perfect: a crewneck pullover, jeans, and an absolutely hideous pair of retro Air Jordans that he had paid an ungodly sum for and, I kid you not, treasured. My indecision about the blanket warped into another, even more intense uncertainty. Was I supposed to kiss him? Or hug him? Or shake his hand like I was president of the Chamber of Commerce? A nervous giggle tried to escape me.

"What's happening right now?" Bobby asked, appraising me.

The giggle tried to slip out. I didn't trust myself to speak, so I shook my head.

"Are you upset?" Bobby asked. "Do you want me to leave?"

"No. No, don't leave. I just didn't—am I supposed to kiss you?"

A distant part of me recognized that Bobby had not, perhaps, realized what he was getting himself into, and he was clearly, at this point, in way over his head.

"Do you want to kiss me?" he finally asked.

"Pretty much always. But, um, not if you don't want me to. I know yesterday was—"

"Yes."

I adjusted the blanket. "Do you want to think about it?"

"No. The answer is yes, you're supposed to kiss me."

"But, like, if—"

"No ifs."

"There are always ifs."

He flexed his hands at his side, and in the tone of a man who knows he's sinking fast, he said, "Dash."

"What if you're a mummy and your face is covered in bandages? What if your lips get burned off in a horrible, um, molten-lava-cake-related disaster? What if we're in *public*?"

The wind stirred the pine and spruce outside, and even through the window, I could hear the creak of their branches.

"Okay," Bobby said, with that same tone.

And he came across the room and kissed me.

(In case you're wondering, somehow in the last few hours, he'd gotten even better.)

"Any more questions?" he asked when he finally let me breathe.

"I know this is hypothetical," I managed breathily, "but what if—"

He kissed me again. One arm was tight around my waist. The other hand was steady on my back. And I wondered if he could feel my heartbeat.

When he stepped back, he shot me an interrogatory look.

By that point, though, I didn't have any questions. I didn't have any brains, as a matter of fact.

Bobby settled me in my favorite chair again. He pulled the hassock over and sat. He was so close that our knees touched, and they bumped again when he raised himself slightly to retrieve something from his back pocket. A packet of folded paper. I recognized his script.

"Oh no," I said (because it turns out when kisses turn to terror, you can't help yourself). "That can't be good."

"Dash," Bobby said, and his voice was strained with emotion I couldn't pin down. "Please."

That didn't do much for my panic, but somehow I managed to nod.

Bobby unfolded the paper and smoothed the sheets against his thigh. His knee began to bounce, and the papers whispered against each other. A furrow creased Bobby's forehead, and his jaw tightened, and a flush climbed his throat and into his cheeks. Deep inside me, a traitorous voice told me this was what he had looked like before he had broken the bad news to West.

Voice rough, he said, "I want to start by telling you that I broke up with Kiefer this morning."

He stopped, clearly waiting for a reaction.

"Um," I said. And then, "Okay, that's good. I mean, is it good? I mean, what about—" Saying *the fact that you told me you're in love with him* didn't seem like the right move, but what came out instead was, somehow, even worse: "—the security deposit on the apartment?"

Although not the eye-rolling type, Bobby looked sorely tempted. His voice, though, was still unsteady when he spoke again. "I also want to apologize. I should have done this a long time ago." He stopped. The pages rustled, and his heel beat a tattoo against the floor. "I told you once how hard it is for me to talk about the things that matter most to me. When I told you that, I couldn't believe how…how easy it was. I just said the words, and I knew you'd understand. And when that happened, I thought it was because you were the exception. I thought you were special. And you *are* special, Dash. I've never met anyone like you. You care so much about other people. You're gentle and kind, even though you're so hard on yourself. You make the world a better place by being in it, and the worst days of my life are when I don't get to be around you, and see your smile, and hear your voice.

"But I also need to apologize, Dash, because you aren't the exception. The truth is, it's still hard for me to talk about—about how I feel. I want to. I know I need to. But it's hard to explain how—"

He stopped there. His throat worked soundlessly on the words, and his eyes glistened as he blinked rapidly.

"Bobby, it's okay," I said.

Shaking his head, he cleared his throat. After another moment, he said, "How scary it is. And after I broke up with West, when I wanted to tell you how hard things had gotten, it was like everything had changed between us. I couldn't tell you anything. And I thought maybe I'd been wrong." He turned the page, and the papers rustled like dry leaves. "It took me a while to realize that I'd felt so safe with you at the beginning because, at the time, West had been there. Between us. And as long as West was there, I didn't have to deal with how I felt about you, or the fact that I found myself spending time with you instead of my boyfriend, or that the more time I spent with you, the more I realized I wasn't in love with West, and I was making a terrible mistake. So, I'm sorry that I let my fear keep me from talking to you.

"You were right about how hard I've tried to run away from my feelings. I'm sorry for that, too. I'm sorry that I used you as one of those ways. That wasn't right. And it wasn't fair to you. I knew you weren't ready, and I still tried to—to control things. To make things be what I needed them to be so that I didn't feel so insecure. The same way I did with West." He had to stop again. His breath was harsh and quick. "The same way I was doing with Kiefer."

"Bobby," I said. "You didn't do that with West. This isn't the same."

He pressed his fingertips to the page, but I could still see them trembling. His eyes met mine. "No," he said quietly. "That's true. This isn't the same. Nothing is the same."

I couldn't think of anything to say. I couldn't think of anything, as a matter of fact, except how brightly his eyes were shining.

"I need you to know I'm sorry," Bobby said, his voice wobbly now, his face strained with the effort to check his emotions. "I need you to know that it's terrifying for me to feel out of control, and nothing makes me feel more out of control than...than feeling this way. How much I feel for you, that scares me. And the thought that something bad could happen to you, that I could lose you, it *terrifies* me. When I saw the Jeep at the bottom of the hill." He stopped. The pages shivered in his hands. "When I stepped into that house and saw that old man pointing a gun at you." He had to stop again, blinking frantically. When he spoke again, his voice was so thick I could barely understand the words. "I can't promise that I'm going to be a different person overnight, but I promise I'll work on this, Dash. On talking. On communicating. On being vulnerable. On making sure you know that you're the most important person in the world to me. I'll do whatever you want, Dash, if you'll please give me a chance."

I was nodding before he'd even finished. And I was crying, although I didn't know why. Wiping my cheeks, I said, "I'll help you. We'll help each other."

He nodded. "I know."

I thought I was done, but fresh tears spilled down my cheeks. I was smiling so hard my face hurt, and the most I could manage was a whisper: "You wrote it down."

"Someone much smarter than me told me it might help," Bobby said. "And he was right. But I didn't write down all of it."

He folded the sheets of paper again and returned them to his pocket. And then he got to his knees. His hands came to rest on my legs, and he looked up at me, and his hands were trembling, and I could hear his breath high in his chest, and a long way off, the ocean was a low, slow song.

"I love you," he said, and his hands tightened around my legs like he was holding on. And then, more slowly, "I love you."

"I love you too," I said, but it came out small and tangled because of the knot in my throat. I started to stand, and I got tangled in the blanket, and then Bobby had to jump to his feet to keep me from falling on him.

And then we were standing again, his hands on my arms, his grip strong and steady.

"I love you," he said again, and he kissed me.

The warmth of his lips. The taste of his mouth. His hand finding the back of my neck.

Sometime later, I was blinking at him through my glasses, trying to decide if I still had legs. And Bobby had that beautifully goofy smile stretched across his face. And then it changed to something else—an expression I hadn't seen on his face before. His hand slid up my chest, and he caught the tab of the hoodie's zipper, and the smile on his face was like a fire about to catch.

"What do you think you're doing?" I asked.

He was looking at me, and that look was new too.

"You're the detective," he said, and I heard the echo, when he had said those words before and meant something else entirely. The zipper stuttered down an inch. "Figure it out."

By the Book

Keep reading for a sneak preview of *By the Book*,
the next book in The Last Picks.

Chapter 1

My phone buzzed with an incoming call—the third one that day.

And, for the third time that day, I hung up on my parents.

It's not technically hanging up, not without a receiver you can slam into a cradle; I know that. But it sounds more dramatic than *I declined the call* or *I sent them to voicemail*.

Seconds trickled past, and my phone stayed quiet. I let my eyes drift back to the laptop screen.

I was sitting in the den at Hemlock House, which I had turned into my office/writing room/occasional napatorium. By a rare bit of luck, I had the late afternoon all to myself. And I was trying to balance my checkbook.

I mean, I hadn't written a check in at least a year, so there weren't a lot of transactions to reconcile. And I was probably missing some obvious piece of information, but I wasn't even sure *why* people balanced their checkbooks in an age when you had instant, online access to all your account records (including your current balance). But—based on the little I knew about finances—balancing a checkbook seemed to be one way to find money. Or at least that's what it looked like in TV shows and movies. People would sit at a table with a gingham tablecloth, and they'd have a pen in one hand, a calculator near their elbow, maybe a cup of coffee. They'd go down each line of the register and add numbers and subtract numbers. And voilà—money!

This was part of being the new, responsible, independent Dash, who was a fully functioning adult and who didn't need anyone to take care of him.

Also, I really, really needed money.

I'd lived in Hastings Rock for over a year now. It had been—even with all the murder and mayhem—the best year of my life. I owned a Class V haunted mansion (okay, that was my own designation, but honestly, Hemlock House was amazing). I had wonderful friends, not counting the time Keme had tried to give me a homemade tattoo with a ballpoint pen. I had met someone I loved more than I'd ever thought possible, and somehow—against all odds—Bobby seemed to love me back. I was even writing again. Well, *again* wasn't the most accurate word. I was writing *consistently* for the first time in my life.

But one of the things they don't tell you about owning a Class V haunted mansion is that they're expensive—expensive to heat, expensive to maintain, and particularly expensive when ordinary household maintenance (say, a leaky roof) gets complicated by factors like, oh, historic preservation.

It wasn't only Hemlock House, though. I hadn't worked—unless you count writing, which nobody considers a real job—since I'd left Providence. I'd blown through my meager savings because, in addition to this money pit, I had other expenses. Like food. I was crazy about food. I wanted to eat it every day. And occasionally getting a haircut so Bobby didn't decide he'd accidentally gotten into a relationship with an unkempt mountain man (is that rude? Should I have said *a grizzled old prospector*?). Plus, a few months before, a very dangerous man had run me off the road. I'd survived with nothing more than some bad scrapes, but the Jeep had been totaled—and I didn't have money to replace it. On top of those concerns, there were other expenses in daily life—like occasionally going out for dinner and drinks with my friends. Or doing something nice for my oh-so-patient, oh-so-understanding, oh-so-handsome boyfriend.

Based on the current balance of my bank account, the only nice thing I was going to be able to do for Bobby in the near future would be buy him a ring pop.

Not that I was thinking about rings. It was too early.

I mean, not that I hadn't at least considered the possibility.

Like, there was this one ring I'd found. It wasn't anything fancy—just a gold band—but I knew from the picture that it would look AMAZING (cue Millie) on Bobby because on top of everything else, he had nice hands, and sometimes he wore a gold chain so I knew gold looked good on him, and of course he'd want something simple and understated and traditionally masculine and—

A door opened and closed, and familiar steps moved toward the den as Bobby called out, "Dash?"

He appeared in the doorway a moment later. He was wearing his running shoes, running shorts, and a tank top that was dark with sweat. His golden-olive skin was a little darker than usual, his shoulders and nose sun-kissed from his time outside. (August on the Oregon Coast is probably the only time anyone around here ever comes close to sun-kissed.) A few damp strands of hair had fallen out of their perfect part and clung to his forehead. My brain immediately decided to roll over and play dead.

"Oh," he said. "You're writing. Sorry."

"No, it's okay. I'm not writing."

"You're not?"

"Uh, actually, I am."

This was apparently grounds for further investigation by Deputy Bobby. He grabbed the door jamb with one hand and, with the other, began to stretch his quad by pulling one leg up and back.

It was, to say the least, distracting.

"Everything okay?" he asked.

"Mmmm."

"Dash?"

"Hm?"

"You're writing? During your writing time?" Bobby switched legs and hammered home with "Like we talked about?"

"Uh huh."

"What are you writing today?"

I blame my brain, which was still playing dead, because I take zero responsibility for what came out of my mouth: "A sex scene."

Bobby's eyebrows went *up*.

"Uh," I said.

He changed stretches. He started pulling one knee up toward his chest.

"Not—I mean, it's not *really* a sex scene."

Bobby switched knees.

"It's more, um, romantic. Tasteful. That's the key word. Tasteful. It's all very tasteful. Plus they're wearing clothes."

He seemed to consider this as he put both feet on the floor again. And then, eyebrows arching once more, he pulled the tank up to mop his face—in the process, exposing his tightly defined abs.

I mean, he was my boyfriend. I was legally obligated to look.

I was looking (and admiring) when my phone buzzed.

I jumped. I said some words that would never have made it into a romantic, tasteful, fully clothed sex scene (whatever that was). My phone buzzed again. I tried to grab it, but apparently all my blood had apparently gone, um, elsewhere, and my hands weren't working, and my phone was *still* buzzing.

Finally, I got hold of it and dismissed the call.

"Was that your parents?" Bobby asked.

"Unfortunately."

"They've been calling all week."

It was a question, even if he was too polite to frame it as one. And unfortunately, after four calls in one day, I was ready to let loose—which was why my response came pouring out.

"Yeah, they've been calling all week because they're trying to make a power play, and they're not happy that I won't go along with it like I usually do."

"What—"

"They just won't—" I said over him.

And right then, my phone began to vibrate.

"—stop calling."

Bobby came across the room as I dismissed the call. "What do you mean, a power play?"

"Nothing. Never mind."

"But you're upset."

"I appreciate the concern, but Bobby, I promise, this is a blip. I've got everything under control—"

My phone buzzed again.

At the same time, the front door crashed open. Millie's voice rang out through the house. "DASH, KASSANDRA AND ANGELINE ARE HOGGING THE BATHROOM, SO I'M GOING TO GET READY HERE." Pause. "DID YOU KNOW THE CHIMNEY LOOKS REALLY SLANTY?"

"What about the chimney?" Bobby asked. "Which chimney?"

"I have no idea," I said as I wriggled past him to make my escape.

"This conversation isn't over, Dash."

By the time I got to the hall, Millie was already halfway to the stairs. Keme was hurrying after her, carrying a toiletry bag, a hair dryer, and several cans, tins, and bottles of various hair products. He glared at us—daring us to make a comment—and then gestured with his chin to the far side of the house before trotting upstairs after Millie.

"Okay," Bobby said, "we definitely need to get that checked out."

"I'll take care of it. Trust me, Bobby, I've got everything under control—"

The lights flickered. And then the power went out.

Bobby didn't say anything. He just breathed out slowly.

"It's probably Millie's hair dryer," I said, but my voice wasn't at a hundred percent.

From upstairs came: "DASH, THE POWER'S OUT AND I DIDN'T EVEN USE MY HAIR DRYER."

In the gloom, Bobby's breathing sounded very loud.

"Uh, that's strange," I said in what I hoped was my most convincingly baffled voice.

"Dash," Bobby said.

I tried not to say anything, but he waited me out. "Yeah?"

"Why is the power off?"

"I don't know?" But it sounded way too much like a question.

The wind wrapped itself around the house, shaking the old shutters.

Finally, in a surprisingly even voice, Bobby asked, "Don't you have an event here tonight?"

I did. In fact, I was hosting an event that most of the town would be attending. Hey, renting out Hemlock House as a venue hadn't gone well the first time—but maybe tonight would be better?

Besides, I was desperate.

All I said, though, was "Yup."

More silence.

"Okay," Bobby said. "I'll—"

"No, Bobby, please. You don't have to do anything. I'm sure it's a misunderstanding. I've got everything under—"

"Don't say it."

"—control."

That was when the front door opened again, and my parents stepped inside.

Acknowledgements

My deepest thanks go out to the following people (in alphabetical order):

Jolanta Benal, for helping me with my blonds, for correcting lie/lay (and sparing me the chart!), and for spotting so many other errors in punctuation, continuity, and more.

Savannah Cordle, for the most amazing live-commentary-read-through, for her excellent questions about what Bobby has told whom, and for reminding me about Dash's phone.

Meg DesCamp, for her expert corrections to the text, for reminding me it was a bombing (not a shooting), and for her help with the bracelet (I really did try to listen!).

Winston Eisiminger, for asking about Candy's sedan, for his kind words about Dash's character development, and for making time to help me with this book when he was incredibly busy.

Austin Gwin, for his question about Dash and Hugo's shared doc, his help with the airbags, and for his feedback on Dash and Bobby's relative responsibility for their current situation.

Marie Lenglet, for her meticulous attention to the text, for fixing so many continuity errors, and for her generous encouragement and enthusiasm for this book.

Brett McMillan, for his expertise (rushes and sedge, metallic smells), for making me laugh (Dashiell Damsell Dane, "too many Ds"), and for his combination threat-slash-plea final comment about Dash and Bobby's future.

Cheryl Oakley, for helping me clean up the manuscript, for her clarifying questions and suggestions, and for asking if Jane divorced Richard.

Meredith Otto, for spotting errors that slipped past everyone else, for her kind words about the cozy-ness of this book, and for her excitement about the next one.

Pepe, for his suggestion about Crocs, for the absolutely *perfect* healed-by-waffles moment, and for his questions about the logistics of the slough.

Nichole Reeder, for her kindness about the swoon-worthy moments, for that vivid detail about the airbags, and for all her help and enthusiasm for this book.

Tray Stephenson, for his help with word choice (definitely not 'opening'), for his help proofing the text, and for his willingness to beta read this book after so many others.

Mark Wallace, for spotting my missing words, for his feedback on the Agatha Christie paragraphs, and for sharing his reader brain (and his teacher brain!).

Wendy Wickett, for her excellent editorial eye (hyphens!), for her patience with my lower-case choices, and for her kind attaboy with regard to the ending.

And special thanks to Alicia, Crystal, Greg, and Raye for their feedback on the ARC.

About the Author

For advanced access, exclusive content, limited-time promotions, and insider information, please sign up for my mailing list at **www.gregoryashe.com**.

Printed in Poland
by Amazon Fulfillment
Poland Sp. z o.o., Wrocław